Selected Stories

ROBERT WALSER

Selected Stories

WITH A FOREWORD BY

Susan Sontag

Translated by
CHRISTOPHER MIDDLETON
and others

FARRAR · STRAUS · GIROUX
NEW YORK

Library of Congress Cataloging in Publication Data
Walser, Robert, 1878–1956.
Selected stories.
I. Title.
PR2647.A64A25   1982   833'.912   82–9257
                                              AACR2

[v]

Contents

Walser's Voice

ROBERT WALSER is one of the important German-language writers of this century—a major writer, both for his four novels that have survived (my favorite is the third, written in 1908, *Jakob von Gunten*) and for his short prose, where the musicality and free fall of his writing are less impeded by plot. This selection of Walser's short prose was made (and mostly translated) by the admirable Christopher Middleton, who has labored for years to make Walser known to English-language readers, and draws from work done between 1907 and 1929.

Anyone seeking to bring Walser to a public that has yet to discover him has at hand a whole arsenal of glorious comparisons. A Paul Klee in prose—as delicate, as sly, as haunted. A cross between Stevie Smith and Beckett: a good-humored, sweet Beckett. And, as literature's present inevitably remakes its past, so we cannot help but see Walser as the missing link between Kleist and Kafka, who admired him greatly. (At the time, it was more likely to be Kafka who was seen through the prism of Walser. Robert Musil, another admirer among Walser's contemporaries, when he first read Kafka pronounced the latter "a peculiar case of the Walser type.") I get a similar rush of pleasure from Walser's single-voiced short prose as I do from Leopardi's dialogues and playlets, that great writer's triumphant short prose form. And the variety of mental weather in Walser's stories and sketches, their elegance and their unpredictable lengths remind me of the free, first-person forms that abound in classical Japanese literature: pillow book, poetic diary, "essays in idleness." But any true lover of Walser will want to disregard the net of comparisons that one can throw over his work.

In long as in short prose Walser is a miniaturist, promulgating the claims of the anti-heroic, the limited, the humble, the small —as if in response to his acute feeling for the interminable. Walser's life illustrates the restlessness of one kind of depressive temperament: he had the depressive's fascination with stasis, and with the way time distends, is consumed; and spent much of his life obsessively turning time into space: his walks. His work plays with the depressive's appalled vision of endlessness: it is all voice—musing, conversing, rambling, running on. The important is redeemed as a species of the unimportant, wisdom as a kind of shy, valiant loquacity.

The moral core of Walser's art is the refusal of power; of domination. I'm ordinary—that is, nobody—declares the characteristic Walser persona. In "Flower Days" (1911), Walser evokes the race of "odd people, who lack character," who don't want to do anything. The recurrent "I" of Walser's prose is the opposite of the egotist's: it is that of someone "drowning in obedience." One knows about the repugnance Walser felt for success—the prodigious spread of failure that was his life. In "Kienast" (1917), Walser describes "a man who wanted nothing to do with anything." This non-doer was, of course, a proud, stupendously productive writer, who secreted work, much of it written in his astonishing micro-script, without pause. What Walser says about inaction, renunciation of effort, effortlessness, is a program, an anti-romantic one, of the artist's activity. In "A Little Ramble" (1914), he observes: "We don't need to see anything out of the ordinary. We already see so much."

Walser often writes, from the point of view of a casualty, of the romantic visionary imagination. "Kleist in Thun" (1913), both self-portrait and authoritative tour of the mental landscape of suicide-destined romantic genius, depicts the precipice on the edge of which Walser lived. The last paragraph, with its excruciating modulations, seals an account of mental ruin as grand as anything I know in literature. But most of his stories and sketches bring consciousness back from the brink. He is just having his "gentle and courteous bit of fun," Walser can assure us, in "Nervous" (1916), speaking in the first person. "Grouches, grouches, one must have them, and one must have the courage to live with them. That's the nicest way to live. Nobody should be afraid of his little bit of weirdness." The longest of the stories, "The Walk" (1917), identifies walking with a lyrical mobility and detachment of temperament, with the "raptures of freedom"; darkness arrives only at the end. Walser's art assumes depression and terror, in order (mostly) to accept it—ironize over it, lighten it. These are gleeful as well as rueful soliloquies about the relation to gravity, in both senses, physical and characterological, of that word: anti-gravity writing, in praise of movement and sloughing off, weightlessness; portraits of consciousness walking about in the world, enjoying its "morsel of life," radiant with despair.

In Walser's fictions one is (as in so much of modern art) always inside a head, but this universe—and this despair—is anything but solipsistic. It is charged with compassion: awareness of the creatureliness of life, of the fellowship of sadness. "What kind of people am I thinking of?" Walser's voice asks in "A Sort of Speech" (1925). "Of me, of you, of all our theatrical little dominations, of the freedoms that are none, of the unfreedoms that are not taken seriously, of these destroyers who never pass up a chance for a joke, of the people who are desolate?" That question mark at the end of the answer is a typical Walser courtesy. Walser's virtues are those of the most mature, most civilized art. He is a truly wonderful, heartbreaking writer.

Susan Sontag

*I am a kind of artisan novelist. A writer of
novellas I certainly am not. If I am well-
disposed, that's to say, feeling good, I tailor,
cobble, weld, plane, knock, hammer, or nail
together lines the content of which people
understand at once. If you liked, you could
call me a writer who goes to work with a lathe.
My writing is wallpapering. One or two kindly
people venture to think of me as a poet, which
indulgence and manners allow me to concede. My
prose pieces are, to my mind, nothing more nor
less than parts of a long, plotless, realistic
story. For me, the sketches I produce now and
then are shortish or longish chapters of a
novel. The novel I am constantly writing is
always the same one, and it might be described
as a variously sliced-up or torn-apart book of
myself.*

ROBERT WALSER, *"Eine Art Erzählung,"*
1928–29

Selected Stories

Response to a Request

You ask me if I have an idea for you, a sort of sketch that I might write, a spectacle, a dance, a pantomime, or anything else that you could use as an outline to follow. My idea is roughly the following: Get hold of some masks, half a dozen noses, foreheads, tufts of hair, and eyebrows, and twenty voices. If possible, go to a painter, who should also be a tailor, and have him make a series of costumes, and be sure to obtain a few good and solid pieces of scenery, so that, wearing a black overcoat, you can walk up some stairs or look out at a window, then utter a roar, a short, leonine, thick, heavy roar, to make people really believe that a soul is roaring, a human heart.

I ask you to attend to this cry, put elegance into it, make it sound pure and right, and then, as you like, you may reach up to one of your tufts of hair and lay it, *doucement*, on the ground. This, if done gracefully, will have a horrifying effect. People will think that pain has made you stupid. In order to obtain a tragic effect, you must employ the nearest as well as the remotest means; I say this so that you'll now understand that it would be good, next, to put your finger into your nose and pick around with it vigorously. Some spectators will weep when they see this, such a noble, somber figure as yours, behaving so rudely and deplorably. It depends on what sort of face you make and from which angle the light shines on you. Be sure to dig your electrician in the ribs so that he'll take the right amount of trouble, and above all coordinate your features, your gestures, your arms, legs, and mouth.

Remember what I told you before; namely—and you'll know it still, I hope—that it is possible for one eye alone, open or closed, to achieve an effect of terror, beauty, grief, or love, or what have you. It doesn't take much to show love, but at some time or another in your, praise God, disastrous life you must have felt, honestly and simply, what love is and how love likes to behave. It is the same, naturally, with anger also, and with feelings of speechless grief; briefly, with every human feeling. Incidentally, I advise you to perform athletic exercises often in your room, to go for walks in the forest, to fortify the wings of your lungs, to practice sports, but only select and balanced sports, to go to the circus and observe the behavior of the clowns, and then seriously to consider by which rapid movements of your body you can best render a spasm of the soul. The stage is the open, sensual throat of poetry, and, dear sir, it is your legs that can strikingly manifest quite definite states of the soul, not to mention your face and its thousand mimings. You must take possession of your hair, if, in order to manifest fright, it is to stand on end, so that the spectators, who are bankers and grocers, will gaze at you in horror.

So now you will have been speechless, will have, lost in thought, picked your nose like a rude and unthinking child, and now you begin to speak. But as you are about to do so, a greenish fiery snake crawls and licks its way out of your pain-contorted mouth, which makes all your limbs seem to tremble with dread. The snake falls to the ground and coils itself around the tranquil tuft of hair, a shriek of fright as from one single mouth goes through the whole auditorium; but already you are offering something new, you stick a long curved knife into one eye, so that the knife's point, dripping with blood, appears from the lower part of your neck, near the throat; after this, you light a cigarette and behave in a curiously cozy way, as if you were privately amused about something. The blood that soils your body becomes stars, the stars dance around the whole stage area, burning and wild, but then you catch them all in your open mouth, and make them disappear, one by one. This will have brought your theatrical art essentially to a degree of perfection. Then the painted-scenery houses collapse, like frightful drunkards, and bury you. Only one of your hands is to be seen, reaching up from the smoking ruins. The hand is still moving a little, then the curtain descends.

[1907]

Flower Days

O N Cornflower Day, when everyone struts around in blue, it became evident how much the writer of the present scientific treatise feels himself to be a good, innocent child of his times. Indeed, I have participated in each and every nice and nasty cornflower folly with joy, love, and delight, and I must have behaved, I believe, very funnily. Several proud and earnest nonparticipants cast severe looks in my direction, but me, happy me, I was as if intoxicated, and I made a pilgrimage, I must confess, while blushing, from one distillery to the next, while buying, all along the way from Münzstrasse to Motz- strasse, patriotic flowers. Clad in blue from head to foot, I seemed to myself most graceful, but what is more, I felt myself most vividly to be a respectable member of the upper classes. Oh, this sweet feeling, how it befogged me and how happy it makes me, the beautiful, yes perhaps even, depending on cir- cumstances, noble thought that I might fling to left and right, with very graceful gestures, pennies, healthy, true, honest, honorable, well-behaved, good pennies, thereby accomplishing a goodly work. Now come what may, let it happen to me, poor devil that I am: I am pleased with myself, thoroughly so, and a feeling of peace has overcome me, I cannot express it in carefully chosen or unchosen words. In my hand, or fist, I held a thick, huge, and evidently imposing bouquet of freshly picked paper flowers, the fragrance of which captivated me. I discovered, by the way, that such flowers are sold at seven pennies a dozen. A waiter, as honest as he is stupid, who always says "Very well" when he takes an order, told me this in a series of mysterious whispers. I am always on an intimate footing with waiters and suchlike people. That's just by the way.

As for flower days in general, I would have to be a heartless rascal not to grasp at once the noble purport on which they rest, and therefore I leap forward as rapidly as possible and exclaim aloud: Yes, it is true, flower days are heavenly. They are not comical in the least, but have, to my feeling, a thoroughly noble and earnest character. Among us blokes or fellow beings, of course, there are still a few isolated and, it would seem, obstinate people who would scorn to wear, on a flower day, a day of peace and joy, a pleasure flower in their soul-buttonhole. We might hope that such people may soon learn better and nobler ways. As for me, as I may fortunately declare, I am radiant on flower days, with sheer flowery and flowerish satisfaction, and I am one of the most flower-encrusted persons among all those who are beautified, adorned, and beflowered. In a word, on such a Day of Plants I am like a swaying, tender plant, and on the charming Violet Day that soon is coming I shall, this I know for certain, appear in the world myself as a modest and secluded violet. For some magnanimous purpose I might even be able to transform myself into a daisy. In future, let anyone, I would here heartily plead, stick and wedge his buttercup between his lips, whether they be opened or grimly tight shut. Ears, too, are excellent props for flowers. On Cornflower Day I had stuck a cornflower behind each of my three ears, and it was most becoming. Ravishing, too, are roses, and the Rose Days soon to come. Let them descend upon me, those distinctive days, and I shall embellish my home with roses, and, sure as I'm a modern man and understand my epoch, I shall stick a rose in my nose. I can warm to daisy days most animatedly too, since any random fashion, absolutely any, makes of me a servant, a slave, or subject. Yet I am happy so.

Well, even then, such odd people, who lack character, have also to exist. The main thing is: I mean to enjoy my morsel of life as well and as long as I can, and if a person finds it amusing he'll heartily go along with any kind of nonsense; but now I turn to the most beautiful subject of all—to women. For them, for them alone, the gracious flower days were invented, composed, poeticized. If a man wallows in flowers, it's a bit unnatural; but in every way it befits a woman to put flowers in her hair and bring flowers to a man. Such a lady or virgin flower has only to make a sign, a gesture, and at once I hurl myself at her feet, ask her, my whole body trembling with joy, how much the flower costs, and I buy it from her. Then all pale in the face I breathe a glowing kiss upon her roguish little hand, and am prepared to surrender my life for her. Yes, indeed, in this manner, and others to match, I do behave on flower days. From time to time, to refresh myself, I plunge, it is true, into a snack hall and gulp down, there and then, a potted meat sandwich. I adore potted meat, but I adore flowers too. There are now many things that I adore. All the same, one has to do one's duty as a citizen, nobody should make a face, nobody think he has a right to pass the flower days off with a quiet smile. They are a fact of life; but one should respect facts. Should one really?

[1911]

Trousers

I AM thrilled to be writing a report on such a delicate subject as trousers, and thus to be licensed to plunge into medi-
tation upon them; even as I write, a desirous grin, I can feel it, is
spreading over my entire face. Women are, and always will be,
so delicious. Well then, as regards fashion in trousers, tending
as it does to excite all hearts and minds, and to quicken every
pulse, that fashion must conduct the thought of any earnestly
thinking man above all toward that which it accentuates and
importantly clothes: the leg. The leg of the woman is thereby,
to some extent, moved into a more luminous foreground. Anyone who loves, esteems, and admires women's legs, as I do, can
consequently, it would seem, only concur with such a fashion,
and indeed I do concur with it, although I am actually very
much in favor of skirts also. A skirt is noble, awe-inspiring, and
has a mysterious character. Trousers are incomparably more
indelicate and they suffuse the masculine soul, to some extent,
with a shudder. Again, on the other hand, why should horror
not grip us modern people, slightly? It seems to me that we do
very much need to be woken up, to be given a shake.

Yet, if the world went all my way, as is fortunately not yet
the case, to my great gratification (for what then should I do,
poor man that I am!), trousers would be significantly tighter,

so that against the soft, rounded flesh of the leg their material would press very closely, or, to phrase it with more elegance, nestle. For me that would be fashion's triumph, and I would die of delight, or at least hit the floor in a swoon, if ever such a transformation occurred in the domain where ladies' clothing is the question. All the same, it seems to me that this is the limit to which we have come, and, as for us discarded and regrettable lords of creation, we are entitled to anticipate excitedly what is still to come. I imagine that something is to come. A change is now on the way, no question; we men have obviously lost the edge, so the women are taking it over, and indeed, they have already begun, in trousers which still provisionally, to be sure, resemble skirts, to trample around before our very eyes. Knickerbockers! There's something Asiatic about them, something Turkish, something, I must confess, without charm. Turks' trousers and Turks' turbans possess little charm for me. But still I think we may have in store for us a flowering and perfection of trousers. Trousers are still not quite trousers enough. The way they now are, they signify mere silliness. They are essentially too reticent, too embarrassed. O womenfolk, listen, you must: If you really want to impress us men, be more saucy, brazen, and complete in your trouserish, trouserly, and trouserful demands! Sweet ladies! Surely on the streets and in the city squares they will trouser around one day quite differently.

To resume: it is a shame that skirts should now propose to disappear, and that our cultural feelings should be outraged. What's this? one asks. Has Paris run out of midriff ideas? As regards ideas, Paris seems to have become poverty-stricken. It's a terrible shame, the demise of that wondrous Paris of the Senses and of the Dreams. Paris is no more. For that is the whole point. The trouser fashion knows nothing of the midriff. If ever there was something about a woman that was beautiful and captivating to the senses, it was the midriff, uniquely; and precisely this most delicious feature is now absent. To trousers, unconditionally, a midriff must appertain. Something must go through me like a knife, and what's more, it must expand upward and downward. There must be tension in it. At present, women no longer have backs. The wonderful, tumescent, as it were smoothed, back of woman has vanished. This is deplorable. Form! Women no longer have a healthy will to form; they no longer desire to display anything, and the desistence of this desire is the plainest proof that they are in rebellion, that they despise us lords and masters. Anybody whom I try and strive to please is felt by me to be my master. It is too obvious. Of such and similar matters consists the secret of the trouser-skirt: rebellion, dissent, compromise, and insistence on a position to be held. Oh, deplorable, a pitiful situation. Men, men, what a disgraceful defeat you have suffered.

Yet—just a whisper in your ear: into that defeat the woman is also dragged, the trouseress, and this great umbrageous defeat of both sexes means—a lessening of mutual attraction! The women want to make themselves miserable by compelling men to see them as comrades, as trouser-buddies. That's how it is, and it is very sad, the heart informs us. What's more, trouser-dom impinges closely upon the problem of the political activation of women. In trousers the poor dears can stride much more comfortably to the voting booth. They are deceived, ah, the poor dears, if only they knew how heartrendingly boring it is to have the vote. They want to assassinate themselves. So be it. For a chivalrous man there's nothing left to do but bury his head desperately in his hands and wish that the blow might fall upon him. This is the quintessence and the consequence of trousers. Frightful!

[1911]

Two Strange Stories

The Man with the Pumpkin Head

ONCE there was a man and on his shoulders he had, instead of a head, a hollow pumpkin. This was no great help to him. Yet he still wanted to be Number One. That's the sort of person he was. For a tongue he had an oak leaf hanging from his mouth, and his teeth were cut out with a knife. Instead of eyes, he had just two round holes. Back of the holes, two candle stumps flickered. Those were his eyes. They didn't help him see far. And yet he said his eyes were better than anyone's, the braggart. On his pumpkin head he wore a tall hat; used to take it off when anyone spoke to him, he was so polite. Once this man went for a walk. But the wind blew so hard that his eyes went out. He wanted to light them up again, but he had no matches. He started to cry with his candle ends, because he couldn't find his way home. So now he sat there, held his pumpkin head between his hands, and wanted to die. But dying didn't come to him so easily. First there had to come a June bug, which ate the oak leaf from his mouth; there had to come a bird, which pecked a hole in his pumpkin skull; there had to come a child, who took away the two candle stumps.

Then he could die. The bug is still eating the leaf, the bird is pecking still, and the child is playing with the candle stumps.

The Maid

A RICH lady had a maid and this maid had to look after her child. The child was as delicate as a moonbeam, pure as freshly fallen snow, and as lovable as the sun. The maid loved the child as much as she loved the moon, the sun, almost as much as her own dear God Himself. But one day the child got lost, nobody knew how, and so the maid went looking for it, looked for it everywhere in the world, in all the cities and countries, even Persia. Over there in Persia the maid came one night to a broad dark tower, it stood by a broad dark river. But high up in the tower a red light was burning, and the faithful maid asked this light: Can you tell me where my child is? It got lost and for ten years I have been looking for it. Then go on looking for another ten years, said the light, and it went out. So the maid looked for the child another ten years, in all the parts and on all the bypaths of the earth, even in France. In France there is a great and splendid city, called Paris, and to this city she came. One evening she stood by the entrance to a beautiful garden, wept, because she could not find the child, and took out her red handkerchief to wipe her eyes. Then suddenly the garden opened and her child came out. She saw it and died of joy. Why did she die? Did that do her any good? Yet she was old now and could not endure so much any more. The child is now a grand and beautiful lady. If you should ever meet her, give her my best regards.

[1913]

Balloon Journey

T HE three people, the captain, a gentleman, and a young girl, climb into the basket, the anchoring cords are loosed, and the strange house flies, slowly, as if it had first to ponder something, upward. "Bon voyage," shout the people gathered below, waving hats and handkerchiefs. It is ten o'clock in the evening. The captain pulls a map from a case and asks the gentleman if he would like to do the map reading. The map can be read, comparisons made, everything to be seen can be clearly seen. Everything has an almost brownish clarity. The beautiful moonlit night seems to gather the splendid balloon into invisible arms, gently and quietly the roundish flying body ascends, and now, hardly so that one might notice, subtle winds propel it northward. The map-reading gentleman tosses, from time to time, as directed by the captain, a handful of ballast into the depth below. There are five sacks of sand on board, and they must be used sparingly. How beautiful it is, the round, pale, dark depth below. The moonlight, tender and evocative, picks the rivers out, silver. One can see houses down there, so small, like innocuous toys. The forests seem to be chanting somber and ancient songs, but this chanting strikes one as being more like a noble silent knowledge. The earth's image has the features of a huge sleeping man, at least that is

what the youthful girl dreams; she lets her bewitching hand
hang indolently over the rim of the basket. Obeying a whim,
the cavalier is wearing a medieval plumed hat, but is otherwise
dressed in a modern way. How quiet the earth is! One can see
everything distinctly, the particular people in the village
streets, the church spires; tired after a long day's work, the
laborers trampling across the farmyard; the ghostly railroad
streaking by, the dazzling long, white turnpike. Human sorrow,
familiar or unknown, seems to send murmurs up from below.
The loneliness of remote regions has a special tone, such that
one believes one ought to understand and even see this special
thing that slips away from thought. Wondrously now the three
people are dazzled as they see in the glory of its colors the
luminous course of the Elbe. The nocturnal river draws from
the girl a low cry of longing. What might she be thinking of?
From a posy she has brought along with her she pulls a dark
rose, in full bloom, and throws it into the sparkling water. How
sadly her eyes shine as she does so! It is as if the young woman
had just now forever shed a painful conflict. It is a very painful
thing, having to part company with what torments you. And
how mute the world is! Far off, the lights of a major town are
glittering; the canny captain pronounces its name. Beautiful,
enticing depth! Countless areas of field and forest are now behind them, it is midnight. Somewhere on the solid ground now
a thief prowls, hunting for swag, there is a burglary, and all
these people down there, in their beds, this great sleep slept by
millions. An entire earth is dreaming now, and a people rests
from its labors. The girl smiles. And how warm it is, as if one
were sitting in a room, just like home, with mother, aunt, sister,
brother, or with one's lover, lamplit, and reading from a beautiful but rather monotonous long story. The girl wants to sleep;
looking at things has made her quite tired now. The two men
standing in the basket gaze silently but resolutely into the
night. Remarkably white, polished-looking, plateaus alternate
with gardens and small wildernesses of bush. One peers down
into regions where one's feet would never, never have trod,
because in certain regions, indeed in most, one has no purpose

whatever. How big and unknown to us the earth is, thinks the
feather-hatted gentleman. Yes, your own country does finally
become intelligible from up here, looking down. You feel how
unexplored and powerful it is. Two provinces they have now
crossed, and the dawn is coming. Below in the villages human
life wakens again. "What's the name of this place?" the leader
shouts downward. A boy's clear voice replies. And still the two
men are gazing; now, too, the girl is awake again. Colors appear and things become more distinct. One sees lakes inside
their drawn contours, wondrously secluded among forests; one
glimpses ruins of old bastions towering up through old foliage;
hills rise almost imperceptibly, one sees swans trembling and
pale on waters, and the human voices become pleasantly
audible, and onward one flies, onward, and finally the glorious
sun appears, and, attracted by this proud star, the balloon soars
upward into a magical dizzy height. The girl shrieks with fear.
The men laugh.

[1913]

Kleist in Thun

KLEIST found board and lodging in a villa near Thun, on an island in the river Aare. It can be said today, after more than a hundred years, with no certainty of course, but I think he must have walked across a tiny bridge, ten meters in length, and have pulled a bell rope. Thereupon somebody must have come sliding lizardlike down the stairs inside, to see who was there. "Have you a room to let?" Briefly then Kleist made himself comfortable in the three rooms which, at an astonishingly low price, were assigned to him. "A charming local Bernese girl keeps house for me." A beautiful poem, a child, a heroic deed; these three things occupy his mind. Moreover, he is somewhat unwell. "Lord knows what is wrong. What is the matter with me? It is so beautiful here."

He writes, of course. From time to time he takes the coach to Berne, meets literary friends, and reads to them whatever he has written. Naturally they praise him to the skies, yet find his whole person rather peculiar. He writes *The Broken Jug*. But why all the fuss? Spring has come. Around Thun the fields are thick with flowers, fragrance everywhere, hum of bees, work, sounds fall, one idles about; in the heat of the sun you could go mad. It is as if radiant red stupefying waves rise up in his head whenever he sits at his table and tries to write.

He curses his craft. He had intended to become a farmer when he came to Switzerland. Nice idea, that. Easy to think up, in Potsdam. Poets anyway think up such things easily enough. Often he sits at the window.

Possibly about ten o'clock in the morning. He is so much alone. He wishes there was a voice beside him; what sort of voice? A hand; well, and? A body? But what for? Out there lies the lake, veiled and lost in white fragrance, framed by the bewitching unnatural mountains. How it all dazzles and disturbs. The whole countryside down to the water is sheer garden, it seems to seethe and sag in the bluish air with bridges full of flowers and terraces full of fragrance. Birds sing so faintly under all the sun, all the light. They are blissful, and full of sleep. His elbow on the windowsill, Kleist props his head on his hand, stares and stares and wants to forget himself. The image of his distant northern home enters his mind, his mother's face he can see clearly, old voices, damn it all—he has leapt up and run out into the garden. There he gets into a skiff and rows out over the clear morning lake. The kiss of the sun is indivisible, unabating. Not a breath. Hardly a stir. The mountains are the artifice of a clever scene painter, or look like it; it is as if the whole region were an album, the mountains drawn on a blank page by an adroit dilettante for the lady who owns the album, as a souvenir, with a line of verse. The album has pale green covers. Which is appropriate. The foothills at the lake's edge are so half-and-half green, so high, so fragrant. La la la! He has undressed and plunges into the water. How inexpressibly lovely this is to him. He swims and hears the laughter of women on the shore. The boat shifts sluggishly on the greenish, bluish water. The world around is like one vast embrace. What rapture this is, but what an agony it can also be.

Sometimes, especially on fine evenings, he feels that this place is the end of the world. The Alps seem to him to be the unattainable gates to a paradise high up on the ridges. He walks on his little island, pacing slow, up and down. The girl hangs out washing among the bushes, in which a light gleams, melodious, yellow, morbidly beautiful. The faces of the snow-crested mountains are so wan; dominant in all things is a final, intangible beauty. Swans swimming to and fro among the rushes seem caught in the spell of beauty and of the light of dusk. The air is sickly. Kleist wants a brutal war, to fight in battle; to himself he seems a miserable and superfluous sort of person.

He goes for a walk. Why, he asks himself with a smile, why must it be he who has nothing to do, nothing to strike at, nothing to throw down? He feels the sap and the strength in his body softly complaining. His entire soul thrills for bodily exertion. Between high ancient walls he climbs, down over whose gray stone screes the dark green ivy passionately curls, up to the castle hill. In all the windows up here the evening light is aglow. Up on the edge of the rock face stands a delightful pavilion, he sits here, and lets his soul fly, out and down into the shining holy silent prospect. He would be surprised if he were to feel well now. Read a newspaper? How would that be? Conduct an idiotic political or generally useful debate with some respected official half-wit or other? Yes? He is not unhappy. Secretly he considers happy alone the man who is inconsolable: naturally and powerfully inconsolable. With him the position is one small faint shade worse. He is too sensitive to be happy, too haunted by all his irresolute, cautious, mistrusted feelings. He would like to scream aloud, to weep. God in heaven, what is wrong with me, and he rushes down the darkening hill. Night soothes him. Back in his room he sits down, determined to work till frenzy comes, at his writing table. The light of the lamp eliminates his image of his whereabouts, and clears his brain, and he writes now.

On rainy days it is terribly cold and void. The place shivers at him. The green shrubs whine and whimper and shed rain tears for some sun. Over the heads of the mountains drift monstrous dirty clouds like great impudent murderous hands over foreheads. The countryside seems to want to creep away and hide from this evil weather, to shrivel up. The lake is leaden and bleak, the language of the waves unkind. The storm wind,

wailing like a weird admonition, can find no issue, crashes from
one scarp to the next. It is dark here, and small, small. Everything is pressed right up against one's nose. One would like to
seize a sledgehammer and beat a way out of it all. Get away
there, get away!

The sun shines again, and it is Sunday. Bells are ringing. The
people are leaving the hilltop church. The girls and women in
tight black laced bodices with silver spangles, the men dressed
simply and soberly. They carry prayer books in their hands,
and their faces are peaceful, beautiful, as if all anxiety were
vanished, all the furrows of worry and contention smoothed
away, all trouble forgotten. And the bells. How they peal out,
leap out with peals and waves of sound. How it glitters and
glows with blue and bell tones over the whole Sunday sun-
bathed little town. The people scatter. Kleist stands, fanned by
strange feelings, on the church steps and his eyes follow the
movements of the people going down them. Many a farmer's
child he sees, descending the steps like a born princess, majesty
and liberty bred in the bone. He sees big-muscled, handsome
young men from the country, and what country, not flat land,
not young plainsmen, but lads who have erupted out of deep
valleys curiously caverned in the mountains, narrow often, like
the arm of a tall, somewhat monstrous man. They are the lads
from the mountains where cornland and pasture fall steep into
the crevasses, where odorous hot grass grows in tiny flat
patches on the brinks of horrible ravines, where the houses are
stuck like specks on the meadows when you stand far below on
the broad country road and look right up, to see if there can
still be houses for people up there.

Sundays Kleist likes, and market days also, when everything
ripples and swarms with blue smocks and the costumes of the
peasant women, on the road, and on the narrow main street.
There, on this narrow street, by the pavement, the wares are
stacked in stone vaults and on flimsy stalls. Grocers announce
their cheap treasures with beguiling country cries. And usually
on such a market day there shines the most brilliant, the hottest,
the silliest sun. Kleist likes to be pushed hither and thither by

the bright bland throng of folk. Everywhere there is the smell of cheese. Into the better shops go the serious and sometimes beautiful countrywomen, cautiously, to do their shopping. Many of the men have pipes in their mouths. Pigs, calves, and cows are hauled past. There is one man standing there and laughing and forcing his rosy piglet to walk by beating it with a stick. It refuses, so he takes it under his arm and carries it onward. The smells of human bodies filter through their clothes, out of the inns there pour the sounds of carousal, dancing, and eating. All this uproar, all the freedom of the sounds! Sometimes coaches cannot pass. The horses are completely hemmed in by trading and gossiping men. And the sun shines dazzling so exactly upon the objects, faces, cloths, baskets, and goods. Everything is moving and the dazzle of sunlight must of course move nicely along with everything else. Kleist would like to pray. He finds no majestic music so beautiful, no soul so subtle as the music and soul of all this human activity. He would like to sit down on one of the steps which lead into the narrow street. He walks on, past women with skirts lifted high, past girls who carry baskets on their heads, calm, almost noble, like the Italian women carrying jugs he has seen in paintings, past shouting men and drunken men, past policemen, past schoolboys moving with their schoolboy purposes, past shadowy alcoves which smell cool, past ropes, sticks, foodstuffs, imitation jewelry, jaws, noses, hats, horses, veils, blankets, woolen stockings, sausages, balls of butter, and slabs of cheese, out of the tumult to a bridge over the Aare, where he stops, and leans over the rail to look down into the deep blue water flowing wonderfully away. Above him the castle turrets glitter and glow like brownish liquid fire. This might almost be Italy.

At times on ordinary weekdays the whole small town seems to him bewitched by sun and stillness. He stands motionless before the strange old town hall, with the sharp-edged numerals of its date cut in the gleaming white wall. It is all so irretrievable, like the form of a folk song the people have forgotten. Hardly alive, no, not alive at all. He mounts the enclosed wooden stair to the castle where the old earls lived, the

wood gives off the odor of age and of vanished human des-
tinies. Up here he sits on a broad, curved, green bench to enjoy
the view, but closes his eyes. It all looks so terrible, as if asleep,
buried under dust, with the life gone out of it. The nearest
thing lies as in a faraway veil-like dreaming distance. Everything is sheathed in a hot cloud. Summer, but what sort of a
summer? I am not alive, he cries out, and does not know where
to turn with his eyes, hands, legs, and breath. A dream. Nothing there. I do not want dreams. In the end he tells himself he
lives too much alone. He shudders, compelled to admit how
unfeeling is his relation to the world about him.

Then come the summer evenings. Kleist sits on the high
churchyard wall. Everything is damp, yet also sultry. He opens
his shirt, to breathe freely. Below him lies the lake, as if it had
been hurled down by the great hand of a god, incandescent
with shades of yellow and red, its whole incandescence seems
to glow up out of the water's depths. It is like a lake of fire. The
Alps have come to life and dip with fabulous gestures their
foreheads into the water. His swans down there circle his quiet
island, and the crests of trees in dark, chanting, fragrant joy
float over—over what? Nothing, nothing. Kleist drinks it all in.
To him the whole dark sparkling lake is the cluster of di-
amonds upon a vast, slumbering, unknown woman's body. The
lime trees and the pine trees and the flowers give off their
perfumes. There is a soft, scarcely perceptible sound down
there; he can hear it, but he can also see it. That is something
new. He wants the intangible, the incomprehensible. Down on
the lake a boat is rocking; Kleist does not see it, but he sees the
lanterns which guide it, swaying to and fro. There he sits, his
face jutting forward, as if he must be ready for the death leap
into the image of that lovely depth. He wants to perish into the
image. He wants eyes alone, only to be one single eye. No,
something totally different. The air should be a bridge, and the
whole image of the landscape a chair back to relax against,
sensuous, happy, tired. Night comes, but he does not want to
go down, he throws himself on a grave that is hidden under
bushes, bats whiz around him, the pointed trees whisper as soft

airs pass over them. The grass smells so delicious, blanketing the skeletons of buried men. He is so grievously happy, too happy, whence his suffocation, his aridity, his grief. So alone. Why cannot the dead emerge and talk a half hour with the lonely man? On a summer night one ought really to have a woman to love. The thought of white lustrous breasts and lips hurls Kleist down the hill to the lakeside and into the water, fully dressed, laughing, weeping.

Weeks pass, Kleist has destroyed one work, two, three works. He wants the highest mastery, good, good. What's that? Not sure? Tear it up. Something new, wilder, more beautiful. He begins *The Battle of Sempach*, in the center of it the figure of Leopold of Austria, whose strange fate attracts him. Meanwhile, he remembers his *Robert Guiscard*. He wants him to be splendid. The good fortune to be a sensibly balanced man with simple feelings he sees burst into fragments, crash and rattle like boulders collapsing down the landslip of his life. He helps him nevertheless, now he is resolute. He wants to abandon himself to the entire catastrophe of being a poet: the best thing is for me to be destroyed as quickly as possible.

What he writes makes him grimace: his creations miscarry. Toward autumn he is taken ill. He is amazed at the gentleness which now comes over him. His sister travels to Thun to bring him home. There are deep furrows in his cheeks. His face has the expression and coloring of a man whose soul has been eaten away. His eyes are more lifeless than the eyebrows over them. His hair hangs clotted in thick pointed hanks over his temples, which are contorted by all the thoughts which he imagines have dragged him into filthy pits and into hells. The verses that resound in his brain seem to him like the croakings of ravens; he would like to eradicate his memory. He would like to shed his life; but first he wants to shatter the shells of life. His fury rages at the pitch of his agony, his scorn at the pitch of his misery. My dear, what is the matter, his sister embraces him. Nothing, nothing. That was the ultimate wrong, that he should have to say what was wrong with him. On the floor of his room lie his manuscripts, like children horribly forsaken by father and mother. He lays his hand in his sister's, and is content to look at her, long, and in silence. Already it is the vacant gaze of a skull, and the girl shudders.

Then they leave. The country girl who has kept house for Kleist says goodbye. It is a bright autumn morning, the coach rolls over bridges, past people, through roughly plastered lanes, people look out of windows, overhead is the sky, under trees lies yellowish foliage, everything is clean, autumnal, what else? And the coachman has his pipe in his mouth. All is as ever it was. Kleist sits dejected in a corner of the coach. The towers of the castle of Thun vanish behind a hill. Later, far in the distance, Kleist's sister can see once more the beautiful lake. It is already quite chilly. Country houses appear. Well, well, such grand estates in such mountainous country? On and on. Everything flies past as you look to the side and drops behind, everything dances, circles, vanishes. Much is already hidden under the autumn's veil, and everything is a little golden in the little sunlight which pierces the clouds. Such gold, how it shimmers there, still to be found only in the dirt. Hills, scarps, valleys, churches, villages, people staring, children, trees, wind, clouds, stuff and nonsense—is all this anything special? Isn't it all rubbish, quotidian stuff? Kleist sees nothing. He is dreaming of clouds and of images and slightly of kind, comforting, caressing human hands. How do you feel? asks his sister. Kleist's mouth puckers, and he would like to give her a little smile. He succeeds, but with an effort. It is as if he has a block of stone to lift from his mouth before he can smile.

His sister cautiously plucks up the courage to speak of his taking on some practical activity soon. He nods, he is himself of the same opinion. Music and radiant shafts of light flicker about his senses. As a matter of fact, if he admits it quite frankly to himself, he feels quite well now; in pain, but well at the same time. Something hurts him, yes, really, quite correct, but not in the chest, not in the lungs either, or in the head, what? Nowhere at all? Well, not quite, a little, somewhere so that one cannot quite precisely tell where it is. Which means: it's nothing to speak of. He says something, and then come moments when he is outright happy as a child, and then of course the girl makes a rather severe, punitive face, just to show him a little how very strangely he does fool around with his life. The girl is a Kleist and has enjoyed an education, exactly what her brother has wanted to throw overboard. At heart she is naturally glad that he is feeling better. On and on, well well, what a journey it is. But finally one has to let it go, this stagecoach, and last of all one can permit oneself the observation that on the front of the villa where Kleist lived there hangs a marble plaque which indicates who lived and worked there. Travelers who intend to tour the Alps can read it, the children of Thun read it and spell it out, letter by letter, and then look questioning into each other's eyes. A Jew can read it, a Christian too, if he has the time and if his train is not leaving that very instant, a Turk, a swallow, insofar as she is interested, I also, I can read it again if I like. Thun stands at the entrance to the Bernese Oberland and is visited every year by thousands of foreigners. I know the region a little perhaps, because I worked as a clerk in a brewery there. The region is considerably more beautiful than I have been able to describe here, the lake is twice as blue, the sky three times as beautiful. Thun had a trade fair, I cannot say exactly but I think four years ago.

[1913]

The Job Application

E STEEMED GENTLEMEN,
   I am a poor, young, unemployed person in the business
field, my name is Wenzel, I am seeking a suitable position, and
I take the liberty of asking you, nicely and politely, if perhaps
in your airy, bright, amiable rooms such a position might be
free. I know that your good firm is large, proud, old, and rich,
thus I may yield to the pleasing supposition that a nice, easy,
pretty little place would be available, into which, as into a kind
of warm cubbyhole, I can slip. I am excellently suited, you
should know, to occupy just such a modest haven, for my nature is altogether delicate, and I am essentially a quiet, polite,
and dreamy child, who is made to feel cheerful by people
thinking of him that he does not ask for much, and allowing
him to take possession of a very, very small patch of existence,
where he can be useful in his own way and thus feel at ease.
A quiet, sweet, small place in the shade has always been the
tender substance of all my dreams, and if now the illusions I
have about you grow so intense as to make me hope that my
dream, young and old, might be transformed into delicious,
vivid reality, then you have, in me, the most zealous and most
loyal servitor, who will take it as a matter of conscience to

discharge precisely and punctually all his duties. Large and difficult tasks I cannot perform, and obligations of a far-ranging sort are too strenuous for my mind. I am not particularly clever, and first and foremost I do not like to strain my intelligence overmuch. I am a dreamer rather than a thinker, a zero rather than a force, dim rather than sharp. Assuredly there exists in your extensive institution, which I imagine to be overflowing with main and subsidiary functions and offices, work of the kind that one can do as in a dream? —I am, to put it frankly, a Chinese; that is to say, a person who deems everything small and modest to be beautiful and pleasing, and to whom all that is big and exacting is fearsome and horrid. I know only the need to feel at my ease, so that each day I can thank God for life's boon, with all its blessings. The passion to go far in the world is unknown to me. Africa with its deserts is to me not more foreign. Well, so now you know what sort of a person I am. —I write, as you see, a graceful and fluent hand, and you need not imagine me to be entirely without intelligence. My mind is clear, but it refuses to grasp things that are many, or too many by far, shunning them. I am sincere and honest, and I am aware that this signifies precious little in the world in which we live, so I shall be waiting, esteemed gentlemen, to see what it will be your pleasure to reply to your respectful servant, positively drowning in obedience,

Wenzel

[1914]

The Boat

I THINK I've written this scene before, but I'll write it once again. In a boat, midway upon the lake, sit a man and woman. High above in the dark sky stands the moon. The night is still and warm, just right for this dreamy love adventure. Is the man in the boat an abductor? Is the woman the happy, enchanted victim? This we don't know; we see only how they both kiss each other. The dark mountain lies like a giant on the glistening water. On the shore lies a castle or country house with a lighted window. No noise, no sound. Everything is wrapped in a black, sweet silence. The stars tremble high above in the sky and also upward from far below out of the sky which lies on the surface of the water. The water is the friend of the moon, it has pulled it down to itself, and now they kiss, the water and the moon, like boyfriend and girlfriend. The beautiful moon has sunk into the water like a daring young prince into a flood of peril. He is reflected in the water like a beautiful affectionate soul reflected in another love-thirsty soul. It's marvelous how the moon resembles the lover drowned in pleasure, and how the water resembles the happy mistress hugging and embracing her kingly love. In the boat, the man and woman are completely still. A long kiss holds them captive.

The oars lie lazily on the water. Are they happy, will they be happy, the two here in the boat, the two who kiss one another, the two upon whom the moon shines, the two who are in love?

[1914]

Translated by Tom Whalen

A Little Ramble

I WALKED through the mountains today. The weather was damp, and the entire region was gray. But the road was soft and in places very clean. At first I had my coat on; soon, how-ever, I pulled it off, folded it together, and laid it upon my arm. The walk on the wonderful road gave me more and ever more pleasure; first it went up and then descended again. The mountains were huge, they seemed to go around. The whole mountainous world appeared to me like an enormous theater. The road snuggled up splendidly to the mountainsides. Then I came down into a deep ravine, a river roared at my feet, a train rushed past me with magnificent white smoke. The road went through the ravine like a smooth white stream, and as I walked on, to me it was as if the narrow valley were bending and winding around itself. Gray clouds lay on the mountains as though that were their resting place. I met a young traveler with a rucksack on his back, who asked if I had seen two other young fellows. No, I said. Had I come here from very far? Yes, I said, and went farther on my way. Not a long time, and I saw and heard the two young wanderers pass by with music. A village was especially beautiful with humble dwellings set thickly under the white cliffs. I encountered a few carts, otherwise nothing, and I had seen some children on the highway. We don't need to see anything out of the ordinary. We already see so much.

[1914]

Translated by Tom Whalen

Helbling's Story

MY name is Helbling and I am telling my own story because it would probably not be written down by anybody else. With mankind become sophisticated, there can be nothing curious nowadays about a person, like me, sitting down and starting to write his own story. It is short, my story, for I am still young, and it will not be completed, for I shall probably go on living for a very long time. The striking thing about me is that I am a very ordinary person, almost exaggeratedly so. I am one of the multitude, and that is what I find so strange. I find the multitude strange and always wonder: "What on earth are they all doing, what are they up to?" I disappear, yes, disappear in the mass. When I hurry home at midday, as twelve o'clock strikes, from the bank where I am employed, they are all hurrying with me: this one is trying to overtake another, that one is taking longer strides than another; yet, still one thinks, "They will all reach home," and they do reach home, for among them there is not a single extraordinary person who could happen not to find his way home. I am of medium build and therefore have occasion to be glad that I am neither remarkably short nor irrepressibly tall. I am—if I may use the proper word—moderate. When I eat my lunch, I always think I could eat just as well, or even better, at another place, where it might be jollier, and then I wonder where this might be, some place where livelier conversation goes with better food. I review in my mind all the parts of the town and all the places that I know, until I have located something which might perhaps be for me. In general, I have a high opinion of myself; in fact, I think only of myself, and my one concern is to do myself as proud as can be imagined. Because I come from a good family—my father is a respected businessman in a provincial town—I am quick to find all sorts of faults in things which seem to be coming my way and which I have to take upon myself: I mean, nothing is refined enough for me. I constantly feel that there is about me something delectable, sensitive, fragile, which must be spared, and I consider the others as being not nearly so delectable and refined. How can that be so? It is just as if one were not of coarse enough cut for this life. It is in any case an obstacle which hinders me from distinguishing myself, for, when I have a task to perform, let's say, I always take thought for half an hour, sometimes for a whole one. I reflect and dream: "Should I tackle it, or should I still put off tackling it?" and in the meantime—I feel this—some of my colleagues will have been remarking that I am slothful, whereas in fact I am just too sensitive. Ah, how wrongly one is judged! A task always frightens me, causes me to brush my desk lid over with the flat of my hand, until I notice that I am being scornfully observed, or I twiddle at my cheeks, finger my throat, pass a hand over my eyes, rub my nose, and push the hair back from my forehead, as if my task lay in that, and not in the sheet of paper which lies before me, outspread, on the desk. Perhaps I have taken the wrong profession, and yet I confidently believe that in any profession I would be the same, do the same, and fail in the same way. I enjoy, as a result of my supposed slothfulness, little respect. People call me a dreamer and a lazybones. Oh, what a talent people have for giving the wrong labels! Of course, it is true: I do not particularly like work, because I always fancy that it occupies and attracts my intellect too little. And that is another thing. I do not know if I have intellect, and I can hardly claim to believe that I have,

for often I have been convinced that I behave stupidly whenever I am given a task which requires understanding and
acumen. This, in fact, flummoxes me and makes me wonder if I
belong among the curious people who are clever only when
they fancy themselves to be so, and cease to be clever as soon
as they have to show that they really are. I have a quantity of
clever, beautiful, and subtle thoughts; but as soon as I have to
apply them, they fail me and desert me, and I am left standing
there like an ignorant apprentice. Therefore, I do not like my
work, because on the one hand it is not intellectual enough for
me, and on the other it is all over my head the moment it gets
the least bit intellectual. I am always thinking when I should
not be, and I cannot do so when I am obliged to. For this
double reason I also leave the office a few minutes before
twelve and come back always a few minutes later than the
others—which has given me rather a bad name. But it's all the
same to me, what they say about me, all unspeakably the same.
For instance, I know quite well that they consider me a fool,
but I feel that if they have a right to suppose this then I cannot
prevent them from doing so. Also I do actually look foolish, my
face, conduct, walk, voice, and bearing. There is no doubt
about it—to take one example—that my eyes have a rather
silly expression, which easily misleads people and gives them
a low opinion of my mind. My bearing is rather idiotic, rather
vain, too; my voice sounds odd, as if I myself, the speaker, did
not know that I was speaking, when I am speaking. There is
something sleepy about me, something not-quite-woken-up,
and I have already said that people notice this. I always
smooth my hair down flat on my head, which heightens perhaps my effect of defiant and helpless stupidity. Then I just
stand there, at the desk, and can goggle into the room or out of
the window for half an hour. The pen with which I write, I
hold in my inactive hand. I stand and shift my weight from one
foot to the other, since no greater freedom of movement is
permitted me, look at my colleagues, and do not understand at
all why, in their eyes, which squint at me askance, I am a
pitiful, irresponsible slacker, smile if someone gives me a look,

and dream without a thought in my head. If only I could do that, dream! No, I have no idea what that is. I am always thinking that if I had a lot of money I would not work any more, and am as pleased as a child that I could think this, once the thought has come to an end. The salary which I earn seems to me too small, and I do not consider telling myself that I do not even earn that much by what I do, though I know that I do practically nothing. Curious, I have not the talent to be somewhat ashamed of myself. If someone, a superior for instance, rebukes me, I am intensely outraged, for it wounds me to be rebuked. I cannot bear it, though I tell myself that I have deserved reproof. I believe that I oppose the superior's reprimand in order to prolong conversation with him a little, perhaps half an hour, for then another half hour will have passed, during which at least I shall not have been bored. If my colleagues believe that I am bored, they are right, of course, for I am, terribly. Nothing exciting happens! To be bored and to ponder how I can possibly break the boredom—that is what my real occupation is. I achieve so little that I think, concerning myself: "You achieve actually nothing!" Sometimes I have to yawn, quite unintentionally, opening my mouth, right up at the ceiling, and putting my hand up, slowly to cover the aperture. At once I find it opportune to twirl my mustache with my fingertips, and to drum on the desk, say, with the underside of one of my fingers, just as in a dream. Sometimes all this seems to me like an incomprehensible dream. Then I pity myself and could weep for myself. But, when the dreaminess passes, I should like to throw myself flat on the floor, collapse, hurt myself on the edge of the desk, so as to feel the time-killing pleasure of the pain. My soul is not entirely unpained at my situation, for sometimes I perceive, if I listen closely, a gentle plaintive note of accusation in it, like the voice of my still-living mother, who always thought well of me, the reverse of my father, who has stronger principles than she. But to me my soul is too dark and valueless a thing that I should treasure what it lets me perceive. I think nothing of its note. I think that one listens to the murmur of the soul only because of boredom.

When I stand in the office, my limbs slowly turn to wood, which one longs to set fire to, so that it might burn: desk and man, one with time! Time, that always makes me think. It passes quickly, yet in all its quickness it seems suddenly to curl up, seems to break, and then it's as if there were no time at all. Sometimes one hears it rustling, like a flock of startled birds, or, for instance, in a forest: there I am always hearing time rustle, and that does one good, for then one no longer needs to think. But mostly it is otherwise: so deathly still! Can that be a human life, not to feel that one is moving on, toward the end? My life till now seems to have been fairly empty, and the certainty that it will remain empty gives a feeling of endlessness, a feeling which tells one to go to sleep, and to do only the most unavoidable things. So that is just what I do: I only pretend to work industriously when I detect behind me the smelly breath of my boss, creeping up to surprise me in my slothfulness. The breath which streams from him is his betrayer. The good man always provides me with a little distraction, so I really like him quite a lot. But what causes me to respect my duty and instructions so little? I am a small, pale, timid, weak, elegant, silly little fellow, full of unworldly feelings, and would not be able to endure the rigor of life if things ever went against me. Can the thought of losing my job, if I go on like this, inspire no fear in me? As it seems, it cannot; yet again, as it seems, it can. I am a bit afraid and a bit not afraid, too. Perhaps I am too unintelligent to be afraid; yes, it almost seems that the childish defiance with which I justify myself before my fellow men is a sign of weak-mindedness. But, but: it suits marvelously my character, which always instructs me to act a little out of the ordinary, even if it is to my disadvantage. Thus, for instance, I bring, though it is not allowed, small books into the office, where I slit open the pages and read, without really enjoying the reading. But it makes it look like the elegant obstinacy of a man who is cultivated and wants to be more than the others. I do indeed always want to be more, and I have the zeal of a hunting dog when it comes to seeking distinction. If I read the book and a colleague comes up and asks the question, which is perhaps

quite in order, "What are you reading, Helbling?"—that an-
noys me, because in this case it is proper to show an annoyance
which drives the importunate questioner away. I act uncommonly important when I read, look all around to see if people
are noticing how cleverly someone there is improving his mind
and wits; I slit open page after page at splendid leisure, do not
even read any more but satisfy myself with having assumed the
posture of a person immersed in a book. That is how I am:
harebrained, and all for effect. I am vain, but my satisfaction
with my vanity costs remarkably little. My clothes are of
coarse appearance, but I vary them zealously, for it pleases me
to show my colleagues that I own several suits and have some
taste in my choice of colors. I like to wear green, because it
reminds me of the forests, and I wear yellow on windy, airy
days because yellow is right for wind and dancing. I could be
in error here, perhaps, for people point out how often every day
I am in error. One ends up believing that one is a simpleton.
But what difference does it make whether one is a ninny or a
person worthy of esteem, since the rain falls equally on don-
keys and respectable men. And then the sun! I am happy in the
sun, when twelve has struck, to be walking home, and when it
rains I spread the luxuriant bellying umbrella over myself, so
that my hat, which I greatly treasure, shall not get wet. I treat
my hat very carefully, and it always seems to me that if I can
still touch my hat in my usual gentle manner, then I am still an
altogether lucky person. It gives me particular pleasure to put
it, when a working day is over, cautiously on my head. That is,
for me, always, my favorite end to every day. My life does
indeed consist of mere trivialities. I am always telling myself
that, and that seems so strange to me. I have never found it
right to get enthusiastic about big ideals concerning humanity,
for my disposition is more critical than enthusiastic, on which I
congratulate myself. I am a person who feels degraded when
he meets an ideal man, with long hair, sandals on his naked
legs, apron of skin around his loins, and flowers in his hair. I
smile, with embarrassment, in such cases. To laugh aloud, the
thing one would certainly most like to do, is impossible, also it

is in fact more a cause for annoyance than for laughter, living among people who regard a smooth head of hair like mine with distaste. I like to be annoyed, so I always get annoyed at the least provocation. I often make sarcastic remarks and yet certainly have little need to be malicious toward others, since I know quite well what it means to be grieved by the scorn of others. But that is just it: I observe nothing, learn nothing, and behave just as on the day I left school. There's a good deal of the schoolboy in me, and it will probably remain my constant companion through life. There are said to be people who have no capacity for betterment and no talent for learning from the behavior of others. No, I do not learn, for I find it beneath my dignity to surrender to the urge for education. Besides, I am already educated enough to carry a walking stick in my hand with some grace, and to knot a necktie, and to grasp a spoon with my right hand, and to say, when asked, "Thank you, it was very nice yesterday evening." What more can education make of me? Honestly: I think education would be coming to quite the wrong person. I go for money and comfortable status, that's my urge for education. I seem to be terribly superior to a miner, even if he, if he so wished, could whisk me, with the forefinger of his left hand, into a hole in the earth, where I would get dirty. Strength and beauty among poor people and in modest dress make no impression on me. I always think, when I see a person like that, how well-off people like us are, with our superior position in the world, compared with such a work-raddled fool, and no compassion steals into my heart. Where should I keep a heart? I have forgotten that I have one. Certainly it is sad, but how should I find it proper to feel sorrow? One feels sorrow only when one has lost money, or when one's new hat does not fit well, or when one's holdings on the stock exchange drop, and even then one has to ask if that is sorrow or not, and on closer inspection it is not, it is only a fleeting regret, which vanishes like the wind. It is, no, how can I put it now—it is marvelously strange to have no feelings in this way, not to know at all what an emotion is. Feelings which concern one's own person, everyone has these, and they are at root despicable ones, presumptuous ones if they relate to humanity as a whole. But feelings for particular people? Of course, one sometimes would like to ask oneself about this, one feels something like a slight longing to become a good, compliant person, but when could one manage it? Perhaps at seven in the morning, or some other time? Already on Friday, and right through the Saturday following, I am wondering what to do on Sunday, since on Sunday something always has to be done. I seldom go for a walk alone. Usually I join a group of young people, the way one does; it is quite simple, one simply goes along with them, though one knows that one is rather a boring companion. I take the steamer, for example, across the lake, or go on foot, into the forest, or travel by train to more distant, beautiful spots. Often I accompany girls to a dance, and I have found that the girls like me. I have a white face, beautiful hands, an elegant, fluttering dinner jacket, gloves, rings on my fingers, a cane with silver mountings, clean polished shoes, and a tender Sunday sort of bearing, such a remarkable voice, and about my mouth a peevish trait, which I myself have no words to describe, but which seems to endear me to the girls. When I speak, it is as if a man of some gravity were speaking. Pomposity appeals, there's no doubt about that. As for my dancing, it is like that of a person who has only just taken, and enjoyed, lessons: jaunty, delicate, punctual, precise, but too fast and insipid. There is precision and buoyancy in my dancing, but unfortunately no grace. How could I be capable of grace? But I love to dance, passionately. When I dance I forget that I am Helbling, for I am nothing but a happy floating-in-the-air. Thoughts of the office, with its manifold agonies, would not intrude on me at all. Around me are flushed faces; perfume and brightness of girls' clothes, girls' eyes gaze at me; I am flying: can one imagine oneself happier? Now I have got it: once in the cycle of the week I can be happy. One of the girls whom I always accompany is my fiancée, but she treats me badly, worse than the other ones do. She is not even—and I do certainly notice it—faithful to me, hardly loves me, I suppose, and I, do I love her? I have many faults, which I have candidly disclosed, but here all my faults and inadequacies seem to be forgiven me: I love her. It is my joy, that I may love her and often despair because of her. She gets me to carry her gloves and pink silk sunshade when it is summer; and in winter I am allowed to trot after her in the deep snow, carrying her skates. I do not understand love, but feel it. Good and evil are nothing compared with love, which knows nothing other than or outside of love. How should I express it: worthless and empty as I otherwise am, not everything is lost, for I really am capable of faithful love, although I could have ample scope for infidelity. I go with her in the sunshine, under the blue sky, in a boat, which I row forward, and keep on smiling at her, while she seems to be bored. Yes, I am a very boring person. Her mother has a small, seedy, rather ill-reputed workingman's bar, where I can spend whole Sundays on end, sitting, saying nothing, smiling at her. Sometimes, too, her face comes down to mine so as to let me press a kiss on her mouth. She has a sweet, sweet face. On her cheek there is the scar of an old scratch, which makes her mouth twist a little, but sweetly. She has very small eyes, which twinkle at you craftily as if to say: "I'll show you a thing or two!" Often she sits beside me on the shabby, hard sofa, and whispers in my ear that it really is lovely to be engaged. I seldom know what to say to her, for I am always afraid that it would not be opportune; so I am just silent and yet want badly to say something to her. Once she extended to my lips her small, fragrant ear: Hadn't I got anything to say, something that could only be whispered? I said, trembling, that I did not think so, and then she boxed my ears and laughed as well, but not in a friendly way, no, coldly. She does not get on well with her mother and her little sister, and will not let me be kind to her sister. Her mother has a nose that is red from drinking, and she is a lively little woman, who likes to sit at the table with the men. But my fiancée sits with the men, too. Once she said to me, in a quiet voice: "I'm not chaste any more"; her tone was quite natural, and I had no objection to make. What could I possibly have had to say? With other girls I am brisk, and am even witty in my speech; but with her I sit

dumbly and look at her and follow each of her movements with
my eyes. Each time I sit there until the bar has to close, or even
longer, till she packs me off home. When the daughter is not
there, the mother comes to sit at my table and tries to make me
think of her. I fend it off with a hand and I smile. The mother
hates her daughter, and it is obvious that they hate each other,
for each obstructs the other's intentions. Each wants a husband
and each grudges the husband to the other. When I am sitting,
evenings, on the sofa, all the people who come to the bar notice
that I am the bridegroom-to-be, and everyone has a friendly
word for me, but I really could not care. Beside me, the little
sister, who is still at school, reads in her books, or she does big
tall letters in her writing book, and always she passes it across
to me, so that I can look at what she has done. I have never
taken any notice, normally, of such little creatures, and now all
at once I understand how interesting every little growing creature is. It is because of my love for the other one. An honest
love makes one better and more alert. In winter she tells me:
"It will be lovely in spring when we can walk together along
the garden paths"; and in spring she tells me: "It is boring with
you." She wants to live in a big town when she is married,
because she wants to get something out of life. The theaters
and fancy-dress balls, beautiful costumes, wine, laughing conversation, gay exciting people, that is what she loves, that is
what she longs for. I long for it too, as a matter of fact, but how
it can all be done, I do not know. I told her: "Perhaps by next
winter I shall have lost my job." She looked at me them, open-
eyed, and asked: "Why?" What sort of answer should I have
given her? I certainly cannot with a single stroke show her
what sort of person I am. She would despise me. Till now, she
has always thought of me as a man of some ability, a man, of
course a rather odd and boring one, but still a man with a
position in the world. If I now tell her: "You are wrong, my
position is very shaky indeed," she would have no reason to
want my company any more, seeing all her hopes of me destroyed. I let it go, I am a master in letting things slide, as they
say. Perhaps, if I were a dancing instructor, owner of a restau-

rant, or a theater director, or had some other profession connected with the entertainment of people, then I might have some luck, for I am that sort of person, jaunty, afloat, leg-flinging, light, buoyant, quiet, always making a bow and having a tender emotion, who would do well as a landlord, stage manager, or tailor, or something. Whenever I have a chance to make a bow, I am happy. That helps one, does it not, to give a deep look? I even bow where it is not usual to do so, or when only toadies and imbeciles do, so much in love am I with the procedure. For serious man's work I have not the intellect or the sense, neither ear nor eye nor mind. Nothing in the world could be further from me. I want to make a profit, but it has got to cost me no more than the twinkling of an eye, at most the lazy extending of a hand. Normally, unwillingness to work is not quite natural in men, but it fits me, it suits me, even if this is a sorry garb which suits me so perfectly, and even if the garb's cut is pitiable: why shouldn't I say, "It suits me," when anyone can see for himself that it does, to a T. Unwillingness to work! But I don't want to say any more about it. I am always thinking, too, that it is the fault of the climate, the damp lake air, which prevents me from getting to work, and now, with this knowledge pressing upon me, I am looking for a job in the south, or in the mountains. I could direct a hotel, or manage a factory, or run the counter at a smallish bank. A sunny, open landscape should be able to develop talents in me which till now have been dormant. A greengrocery would not be bad. In any case, I am a person who always believes that great inward gains come through external change. Another climate would produce, also, a different menu for lunch, and perhaps this is what the matter is. Could it really be that I am ill? So much is wrong; I am deficient, actually, in everything. Could it be that I am an unlucky person? Could it be a sort of sickness to concern oneself always, as I do, with such questions? Anyway, it is not quite normal. Today I was ten minutes late again at the bank. I cannot get there on time any more as the others do. I ought really to be quite alone in the world, me, Helbling, and not a single living being besides me. No sun, no culture, me, naked on a high rock, no storms, not even a wave, no water, no wind, no streets, no benches, no money, no time, and no breath. Then, at least, I should not be afraid any more. No more fear and no more questions, and I should not be late any more, either. I could imagine that I was lying in bed, everlastingly in bed! Perhaps that would be the best thing.

[1914]

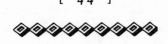

The Little Berliner

PAPA boxed my ears today, in a most fond and fatherly
manner, of course. I had used the expression: "Father,
you must be nuts." It was indeed a bit careless of me. "Ladies
should employ exquisite language," our German teacher says.
She's horrible. But Papa won't allow me to ridicule her, and
perhaps he's right. After all, one does go to school to exhibit a
certain zeal for learning and a certain respect. Besides, it is
cheap and vulgar to discover funny things in a fellow human
being and then to laugh at them. Young ladies should accustom themselves to the fine and the noble—I quite see that.
No one desires any work from me, no one will ever demand
it of me; but everyone will expect to find that I am refined
in my ways. Shall I enter some profession in later life? Of
course not! I'll be an elegant young wife; I shall get married.
It is possible that I'll torment my husband. But that would
be terrible. One always despises oneself whenever one feels
the need to despise someone else. I am twelve years old.
I must be very precocious—otherwise, I would never think
of such things. Shall I have children? And how will that come
about? If my future husband isn't a despicable human being,
then, yes, then I'm sure of it, I shall have a child. Then I shall

bring up this child. But I still have to be brought up myself. What silly thoughts one can have!

Berlin is the most beautiful, the most cultivated city in the world. I would be detestable if I weren't unshakably convinced of this. Doesn't the Kaiser live here? Would he need to live here if he didn't like it here best of all? The other day I saw the royal children in an open car. They are enchanting. The crown prince looks like a high-spirited young god, and how beautiful seemed the noble lady at his side. She was completely hidden in fragrant furs. It seemed that blossoms rained down upon the pair out of the blue sky. The Tiergarten is marvelous. I go walking there almost every day with our young lady, the governess. One can go for hours under the green trees, on straight or winding paths. Even Father, who doesn't really need to be enthusiastic about anything, is enthusiastic about the Tiergarten. Father is a cultivated man. I'm convinced he loves me madly. It would be horrible if he read this, but I shall tear up what I have written. Actually, it is not at all fitting to be still so silly and immature and, at the same time, already want to keep a diary. But, from time to time, one becomes somewhat bored, and then one easily gives way to what is not quite right. The governess is very nice. Well, I mean, in general. She is devoted and she loves me. In addition, she has real respect for Papa— that is the most important thing. She is slender of figure. Our previous governess was fat as a frog. She always seemed to be about to burst. She was English. She's still English today, of course, but from the moment she allowed herself liberties, she was no longer our concern. Father kicked her out.

The two of us, Papa and I, are soon to take a trip. It is that time of the year now when respectable people simply have to take a trip. Isn't it a suspicious sort of person who doesn't take a trip at such a time of blossoming and blooming? Papa goes to the seashore and apparently lies there day after day and lets himself be baked dark brown by the summer sun. He always looks healthiest in September. The paleness of exhaustion is not becoming to his face. Incidentally, I myself love the suntanned look in a man's face. It is as if he had just come home from war. Isn't that just like a child's nonsense? Well, I'm still a child, of course. As far as I'm concerned, I'm taking a trip to the south. First of all, a little while to Munich and then to Venice, where a person who is unspeakably close to me lives— Mama. For reasons whose depths I cannot understand and consequently cannot evaluate, my parents live apart. Most of the time I live with Father. But naturally Mother also has the right to possess me at least for a while. I can scarcely wait for the approaching trip. I like to travel, and I think that almost all people must like to travel. One boards the train, it departs, and off it goes into the distance. One sits and is carried into the remote unknown. How well-off I am, really! What do I know of need, of poverty? Nothing at all. I also don't find it the least bit necessary that I should experience anything so base. But I do feel sorry for the poor children. I would jump out the window under such conditions.

Papa and I reside in the most elegant quarter of the city. Quarters which are quiet, scrupulously clean, and fairly old, are elegant. The brand-new? I wouldn't like to live in a brand-new house. In new things there is always something which isn't quite in order. One sees hardly any poor people—for example, workers—in our neighborhood, where the houses have their own gardens. The people who live in our vicinity are factory owners, bankers, and wealthy people whose profession is wealth. So Papa must be, at the very least, quite well-to-do. The poor and the poorish people simply can't live around here because the apartments are much too expensive. Papa says that the class ruled by misery lives in the north of the city. What a city! What is it—the north? I know Moscow better than I know the north of our city. I have been sent numerous postcards from Moscow, Petersburg, and Holland; I know the Engadine with its sky-high mountains and its green meadows, but my own city? Perhaps to many, many people who inhabit it, Berlin remains a mystery. Papa supports art and the artists. What he engages in is business. Well, lords often engage in business, too, and then Papa's dealings are of absolute refinement. He buys and sells paintings. We have very beautiful paintings in our house. The point of Father's business, I think, is this: the artists, as a rule, understand nothing about business, or, for some reason or other, they aren't allowed to understand anything about it. Or it is this: the world is big and coldhearted. The world never thinks about the existence of artists. That's where my father comes in, worldly-wise, with all sorts of important connections, and in suitable and clever fashion, he draws the attention of this world, which has perhaps no need at all for art, to art and to artists who are starving. Father often looks down upon his buyers. But he often looks down upon the artists, too. It all depends.

No, I wouldn't want to live permanently anywhere but in Berlin. Do the children in small towns, towns that are old and decayed, live any better? Of course, there are some things here that we don't have. Romantic things? I believe I'm not mistaken when I look upon something that is scarcely half alive as romantic. The defective, the crumbled, the diseased; e.g., an ancient city wall. Whatever is useless yet mysteriously beautiful—that is romantic. I love to dream about such things, and, as I see it, dreaming about them is enough. Ultimately, the most romantic thing is the heart, and every sensitive person carries in himself old cities enclosed by ancient walls. Our Berlin will soon burst at the seams with newness. Father says that everything historically notable here will vanish; no one knows the old Berlin any more. Father knows everything, or at least, almost everything. And naturally his daughter profits in that respect. Yes, little towns laid out in the middle of the countryside may well be nice. There would be charming, secret hiding spots to play in, caves to crawl in, meadows, fields, and, only a few steps away, the forest. Such villages seem to be wreathed in green; but Berlin has an Ice Palace where people ice skate on the hottest summer day. Berlin is simply one step ahead of all other German cities, in every respect. It is the cleanest, most modern city in the world. Who says this? Well, Papa, of course. How good he is, really! I have much to learn from him. Our Berlin streets have overcome all dirt and all bumps. They are

as smooth as ice and they glisten like scrupulously polished
floors. Nowadays one sees a few people roller skating. Who
knows, perhaps I'll be doing it someday, too, if it hasn't already
gone out of fashion. There are fashions here that scarcely have
time to come in properly. Last year all the children, and also
many grownups, played Diabolo. Now this game is out of fashion, no one wants to play it. That's how everything changes.
Berlin always sets the fashion. No one is obliged to imitate, and
yet Madam Imitation is the great and exalted ruler of this life.
Everyone imitates.

Papa can be charming; actually, he is always nice, but at
times he becomes angry about something—one never knows—
and then he is ugly. I can see in him how secret anger, just like
discontent, makes people ugly. If Papa isn't in a good mood, I
feel as cowed as a whipped dog, and therefore Papa should
avoid displaying his indisposition and his discontent to his associates, even if they should consist of only one daughter.
There, yes, precisely there, fathers commit sins. I sense it
vividly. But who doesn't have weaknesses—not even one, not
some tiny fault? Who is without sin? Parents who don't consider it necessary to withhold their personal storms from their
children degrade them to slaves in no time. A father should
overcome his bad moods in private—but how difficult that is!
—or he should take them to strangers. A daughter is a young
lady, and in every cultivated sire should dwell a cavalier. I say
explicitly: living with Father is like Paradise, and if I discover
a flaw in him, doubtless it is one transferred from him to me;
thus it is his, not my, discretion that observes him closely. But
Papa may, of course, conveniently take out his anger on people
who are dependent on him in certain respects. There are
enough such people fluttering about him.

I have my own room, my furniture, my luxury, my books,
etc. God, I'm actually very well provided for. Am I thankful to
Papa for all this? What a tasteless question! I am obedient to
him, and then I am also his possession, and, in the last analysis,
he can well be proud of me. I cause him worries, I am his
financial concern, he may snap at me, and I always find it a

kind of delicate obligation to laugh at him when he snaps at me. Papa likes to snap; he has a sense of humor and is, at the same time, spirited. At Christmas he overwhelms me with presents. Incidentally, my furniture was designed by an artist who is scarcely unknown. Father deals almost exclusively with people who have some sort of name. He deals with names. If hidden in such a name there is also a man, so much the better. How horrible it must be to know that one is famous and to feel that one doesn't deserve it at all. I can imagine many such famous people. Isn't such a fame like an incurable sickness? Goodness, the way I express myself! My furniture is lacquered white and is painted with flowers and fruits by the hands of a connoisseur. They are charming and the artist who painted them is a remarkable person, highly esteemed by Father. And whomever Father esteems should indeed be flattered. I mean, it is worth something if Papa is well-disposed toward someone, and those who don't find it so and act as if they didn't give a hoot, they're only hurting themselves. They don't see the world clearly enough. I consider my father to be a thoroughly remarkable man; that he wields influence in the world is obvious. —Many of my books bore me. But then they are simply not the right books, like, for example, so-called children's books. Such books are an affront. One dares give children books to read that don't go beyond their horizons? One should not speak in a childlike manner to children; it is childish. I, who am still a child myself, hate childishness.

When shall I cease to amuse myself with toys? No, toys are sweet, and I shall be playing with my doll for a long time yet; but I play consciously. I know that it's silly, but how beautiful silly and useless things are. Artistic natures, I think, must feel the same way. Different young artists often come to us, that is to say, to Papa, for dinner. Well, they are invited and then they appear. Often I write the invitations, often the governess, and a grand, entertaining liveliness reigns at our table, which, without boasting or wilfully showing off, looks like the well-provided table of a fine house. Papa apparently enjoys going around with young people, with people who are younger than

he, and yet he is always the gayest and the youngest. One hears
him talking most of the time, the others listen, or they allow
themselves little remarks, which is often quite droll. Father
overtowers them all in learning and verve and understanding
of the world, and all these people learn from him—that I
plainly see. Often I have to laugh at the table; then I receive a
gentle or not-so-gentle admonition. Yes, and then after dinner
we take it easy. Papa stretches out on the leather sofa and
begins to snore, which actually is in rather poor taste. But I'm
in love with Papa's behavior. Even his candid snoring pleases
me. Does one want to, could one ever, make conversation all
the time?

Father apparently spends a lot of money. He has receipts
and expenses, he lives, he strives after gains, he lets live. He
even leans a bit toward extravagance and waste. He's constantly in motion. At our house there is much said about success and failure. Whoever eats with us and associates with us
has attained some form of smaller or greater success in the
world. What is the world? A rumor, a topic of conversation? In
any case, my father stands in the very middle of this topic of
conversation. Perhaps he even directs it, within certain bounds.
Papa's aim, at all events, is to wield power. He attempts to
develop, to assert both himself and those people in whom he
has an interest. His principle is: he in whom I have no interest
damages himself. As a result of this view, Father is always
permeated with a healthy sense of his human worth and can
step forth, firm and certain, as is fitting. Whoever grants himself no importance feels no qualms about perpetrating bad
deeds. What am I talking about? Did I hear Father say that?

Have I the benefit of a good upbringing? I refuse even to
doubt it. I have been brought up as a metropolitan lady should
be brought up, with familiarity and, at the same time, with a
certain measured severity, which permits and, at the same
time, commands me to accustom myself to tact. The man who
is to marry me must be rich, or he must have substantial prospects of an assured prosperity. Poor? I couldn't be poor. It is
impossible for me and for creatures like me to suffer pecuniary

need. That would be stupid. In other respects, I shall be certain to give simplicity preference in my mode of living. I do not like outward display. Simplicity must be a luxury. It must shimmer with propriety in every respect, and such refinements of life, brought to perfection, cost money. The amenities are expensive. How energetically I'm talking now! Isn't it a bit imprudent? Shall I love? What is love? What sorts of strange and wonderful things must yet await me if I find myself so unknowing about things that I'm still too young to understand. What experiences shall I have?

[1914]

Translated by Harriett Watts

Nervous

I AM a little worn out, raddled, squashed, downtrodden, shot full of holes. Mortars have mortared me to bits. I am a little crumbly, decaying, yes, yes. I am sinking and drying up a little. I am a bit scalded and scorched, yes, yes. That's what it does to you. That's life. I am not old, not in the least, certainly I am not eighty, by no means, but I am not sixteen any more either. Quite definitely I am a bit old and used up. That's what it does to you. I am decaying a little, and I am crumbling, peeling a little. That's life. Am I a little bit over the hill? Hmm! Maybe. But that doesn't make me eighty, not by a long way. I am very tough, I can vouch for that. I am no longer young, but I am not old yet, definitely not. I am aging, fading a little, but that doesn't matter; I am not yet altogether old, though I am probably a little nervous and over the hill. It's natural that one should crumble a bit with the passage of time, but that doesn't matter. I am not very nervous, to be sure, I just have a few grouches. Sometimes I am a bit weird and grouchy, but that doesn't mean I am altogether lost, I hope. I don't propose to hope that I am lost, for I repeat, I am uncommonly hard and tough. I am holding out and holding on. I am fairly fearless. But nervous I am, a little, undoubtedly I am, very probably I am, possibly I am a little nervous. I hope that I am a little nervous. No, I don't hope so, one doesn't hope for such things, but I am afraid so, yes, afraid so. Fear is more appropriate here than hope, no doubt about it. But I certainly am not fear-stricken, that I might be nervous, quite definitely not. I have grouches, but I am not afraid of the grouches. They inspire me with no fear at all. "You are nervous," someone might tell me, and I would reply cold-bloodedly, "My dear sir, I know that quite well, I know that I am a little worn out and nervous." And I would smile, very nobly and coolly, while saying this, which would perhaps annoy the other person a little. A person who refrains from getting annoyed is not yet lost. If I do not get annoyed about my nerves, then undoubtedly I still have good nerves, it's clear as daylight, and illuminating. It dawns on me that I have grouches, that I am a little nervous, but it dawns on me in equal measure that I am cold-blooded, which makes me uncommonly glad, and that I am blithe in spirit, although I am aging a little, crumbling and fading, which is quite natural and something I therefore understand very well. "You are nervous," someone might come up to me and say. "Yes, I am uncommonly nervous," would be my reply, and secretly I would laugh at the big lie. "We are all a little nervous," I would perhaps say, and laugh at the big truth. If a person can still laugh, he is not yet entirely nervous; if a person can accept a truth, he is not yet entirely nervous; anyone who can keep calm when he hears of some distress is not yet entirely nervous. Or if someone came up to me and said: "Oh, you are totally nervous," then quite simply I would reply in nice polite terms: "Oh, I am totally nervous, I know I am." And the matter would be closed. Grouches, grouches, one must have them, and one must have the courage to live with them. That's the nicest way to live. Nobody should be afraid of his little bit of weirdness. Fear is altogether foolish. "You are very nervous!"

"Yes, come by all means and calmly tell me so! Thank you!"

That, or something like it, is what I'd say, having my gentle and courteous bit of fun. Let man be courteous, warm, and kind, and if someone tells him he's totally nervous, still there's no need at all for him to believe it.

[1916]

The Walk

I HAVE to report that one fine morning, I do not know any more for sure what time it was, as the desire to take a walk came over me, I put my hat on my head, left my writing room, or room of phantoms, and ran down the stairs to hurry out into the street. I might add that on the stairs I encountered a woman who looked like a Spaniard, a Peruvian, or a Creole. She presented to the eye a certain pallid, faded majesty. But I must strictly forbid myself a delay of even two seconds with this Brazilian lady, or whatever she might be; for I may waste neither space nor time. As far as I can remember as I write this down, I found myself, as I walked into the open, bright, and cheerful street, in a romantically adventurous state of mind, which pleased me profoundly. The morning world spread out before my eyes appeared as beautiful to me as if I saw it for the first time. Everything I saw made upon me a delightful impression of friendliness, of goodliness, and of youth. I quickly forgot that up in my room I had only just a moment before been brooding gloomily over a blank sheet of paper. All sorrow, all pain, and all grave thoughts were as vanished, although I vividly sensed a certain seriousness, a tone, still before me and behind me. I was tense with eager expectation of whatever might encounter me or cross my way on my walk. My steps

were measured and calm, and, as far as I know, I presented, as
I went on my way, a fairly dignified appearance. My feelings I
like to conceal from the eyes of my fellow men, of course without any fearful strain to do so—such strain I would consider a
great error, and a mighty stupidity. I had not yet gone twenty
or thirty steps over a broad and crowded square, when Professor Meili, a foremost authority, brushed by me. Incontro-
vertible power in person, serious, ceremonial, and majestical,
Professor Meili trod his way; in his hand he held an unbend-
able scientific walking stick, which infused me with dread,
reverence, and esteem. Professor Meili's nose was a stern, im-
perative, sharp eagle- or hawk-nose, and his mouth was juridi-
cally clamped tight and squeezed shut. The famous scholar's
gait was like an iron law; world history and the afterglow of
long-gone heroic deeds flashed out of Professor Meili's adamant
eyes, secreted behind his bushy brows. His hat was like an
irremovable ruler. Secret rulers are the most proud and most
implacable. Yet, on the whole, Professor Meili carried himself
with a tenderness, as if he needed in no way whatsoever to
make apparent what quantities of power and gravity he per-
sonified, and his figure appeared to me, in spite of all its severity and adamance, sympathetic, because I permitted myself the
thought that men who do not smile in a sweet and beautiful
way are honorable and trustworthy. As is well known, there are
rascals who play at being kind and good, but who have a terrible talent for smiling, obligingly and politely, over the crimes
which they commit.

I catch a glimpse of a bookseller and of a book shop; likewise
soon, as I guess and observe, a bakery with braggart gold let-
tering comes in for mention and regard. But first I have a priest,
or parson, to record. A bicycling town chemist cycles with
kind and weighty face close by the walker, namely, myself,
similarly, a regimental or staff doctor. An unassuming pedes-
trian should not remain unconsidered, or unrecorded; for he
asks me politely to mention him. This is a bric-à-brac vendor
and rag collector who has become rich. Young boys and girls
race around in the sunlight, free and unrestrained. "Let them

be unrestrained as they are," I mused. "Age one day will terrify
and bridle them. Only too soon, alas!" A dog refreshes itself in
the water of a fountain. Swallows, it seems to me, twitter in
the blue air. One or two elegant ladies in astonishingly short
skirts and astoundingly fine high-colored bootees make themselves, I hope, certainly as conspicuous as anything else. Two
summer or straw hats catch my eye. The thing about the straw
hats is this: it is that I suddenly see two hats in the bright,
gentle air, and under the hats stand two fairly prosperous-look-
ing gentlemen, who seem to be bidding each other good morning by means of an elegant, courteous doffing and waving of
hats. The hats at this occasion are evidently more important
than their wearers and owners. Nevertheless, the writer is very
humbly asked to be wary of such definitely superfluous mockery and fooling. He is called upon to behave with sobriety, and
it is hoped that he understands this, once and for all.

As now an extremely splendid, abundant book shop came
pleasantly under my eye, and I felt the impulse and desire to
bestow upon it a short and fleeting visit, I did not hesitate to
step in, with an obvious good grace, while I permitted myself
of course to consider that in me appeared far rather an inspector, or bookkeeper, a collector of information, and a sensitive
connoisseur, than a favorite and welcome, wealthy book buyer
and good client. In courteous, thoroughly circumspect tones,
and choosing understandably only the finest turns of speech, I
inquired after the latest and best in the field of belles-lettres.
"May I," I asked with diffidence, "take a moment to acquaint
myself with, and taste the qualities of, the most sterling and
serious, and at the same time of course also the most read and
most quickly acknowledged and purchased, reading matter?
You would pledge me in high degree to unusual gratitude were
you to be so extremely kind as to lay generously before me that
book which, as certainly nobody can know so precisely as only
you yourself, has found the highest place in the estimation of
the reading public, as well as that of the dreaded and thence
doubtless flatteringly circumvented critics, and which further-

more has made them merry. You cannot conceive how keen I am to learn at once which of all these books or works of the pen piled high and put on show here is the favorite book in question, the sight of which in all probability, as I must most energetically suppose, will make me at once a joyous and enthusiastic purchaser. My longing to see the favorite author of the cultivated world and his admired, thunderously applauded masterpiece, and, as I said, probably also at once to buy the same, aches and ripples through my every limb. May I most politely ask you to show me this most successful book, so that this desire, which has seized my entire being, may acknowledge itself gratified, and cease to trouble me?" "Certainly," said the bookseller. He vanished out of eyeshot like an arrow, to return the next instant to his anxious and interested client, bearing indeed the most bought and read book of real enduring value in his hand. This delicious fruit of the spirit he carried carefully and solemnly, as if carrying a relic charged with sanctifying magic. His face was enraptured; his manner radiated the deepest awe; and with that smile on his lips which only believers and those who are inspirited to the deepest core can smile, he laid before me in the most winning way that which he had brought.

I considered the book, and asked: "Could you swear that this is the most widely distributed book of the year?"

"Without a doubt!"

"Could you insist that this is the book which one has to have read?"

"Unconditionally."

"Is this book also definitely good?"

"What an utterly superfluous and inadmissible question."

"Thank you very much," said I cold-bloodedly, left the book, which had been most absolutely widely distributed because it had unconditionally to have been read, as I chose, where it was, and softly withdrew, without wasting another word. "Uncultivated and ignorant man!" shouted the bookseller after me, for he was most justifiably and deeply vexed. But I let him have his say, and walked at my ease on my way, which, to be accurate, as I shall at once discuss and expound more closely, led into the next stately banking establishment.

The very place I wished to inquire at and receive reliable information about certain securities. "To hop into a money institute, just in passing," I mused, or said to myself, "in order to manage one's financial affairs, and to produce questions, which one utters in no more than a whisper, is pleasant, and looks uncommonly good."

"It is good and wonderfully convenient that you come to us in person," the responsible official at the counter said to me, in a very friendly tone, and he proceeded with an almost knavish, at any rate very charming and gay smile, as follows:

"It is, as I said, good that you have come. Only today we were about to communicate to you in writing what can now be communicated to you orally, namely something which will be for you without a doubt a gladdening piece of information, that we are instructed by a society, or circle, of what are evidently well-disposed, good-natured, philanthropic ladies, not to place to your debit but, on the contrary, and this will doubtless be fundamentally more welcome to you, to credit your account with

One Thousand Francs,

a transaction which we hereby confirm, and of which you, if you would be so good, will at once take mental or any other form of note which may suit you. We assume that this information pleases you; for upon us you make, we must confess, an impression such as tells us, if we may permit ourselves to say so, with almost excessive clarity, that you very definitely need alleviation of an equable and delicate nature. The money is at your disposal with effect from today. One can see that this very minute a great joy suffuses your features. Your eyes are shining; your mouth this minute has about it a trace of laughter, and this perhaps for the first time in many years, for pressing daily troubles of a hideous kind have forbidden you laughter, and you have been perhaps during recent times mostly in a sorrow-

ful mood, since all sorts of evil and sad thoughts darkened your
brow. Now rub your hands for joy, rub them! and be glad that
some noble and kind benefactresses, moved by the sublime
thought that to dam up a man's grief is beautiful, and to allay
his distress is good, conceived the idea that a poor and unsuc-
cessful poet (for you are this, are you not?) might require
assistance. On the fact that certain persons were found whose
will was to condescend to remember you, and on this occasion
of evidence that not all people regard with indifference the
existence of a poet held repeatedly in contempt, we congratulate you."

"The sum of money so unexpectedly bestowed upon me, issuing from such tender and indulgent fairy or ladies' hands," I
said, "I would like to leave without more ado in your charge,
where it will surely be best preserved, since you have at your
disposal the necessary fireproof and thief-tight safes, to keep
your treasures from destruction, or from any abolition whatsoever. Besides, you pay interest. May I ask for a receipt? I assume that I have the liberty to withdraw, at any time according
to my need or desire, from the large sum small sums. I would
like to remark that I am thrifty. I shall know how to manage the
gift like a steady and methodical man; that is, most cautiously.
And I shall have, in a considerate and polite letter, to express
my gratitude to my kind donators, which I think I shall do as
soon as tomorrow morning, so that it does not get forgotten
through procrastination. The assumption, which you just now
voiced so frankly, that I might be poor, could however rest
upon a basis of acute and accurate observation. But it suffices
entirely that I myself know what I know, and that it is I myself
who am best informed about my own person. Appearances
often deceive, good sir, and the delivery of a judgment upon
a man is best left to the man in question. Nobody can know as
well as I do this person who has seen and experienced all sorts
of things. Often I wandered, of course, perplexed in a
mist and in a thousand vacillations and dilemmas, and often I
felt myself woefully forsaken. Yet I believe that it is a fine thing
to struggle for life. It is not with pleasures and with joys that a

man grows proud. Proud and gay in the roots of his soul he
becomes only through trial bravely undergone, and through
suffering patiently endured. Still, on this point, one does not
like to waste words. What honest man was never in his life
without sustenance? And what human being has ever seen as
the years pass his hopes, plans, and dreams completely unde-
stroyed? Where is the soul whose longings and daring aspira-
tions, whose sweet and lofty imaginings of happiness have been
fulfilled without that soul's having had to deduct a discount?"

Receipt for one thousand francs was handed out, or in, to
me, whereupon the steady creditor and accounted competitor,
namely no other than myself, was entitled to bid good day and
to withdraw. My heart glad that this capital sum should fall to
me, magically, as from a blue sky, I ran out of the high and
beautiful vestibule into the open air, to continue my walk.

Add I would, can, and I hope may (since nothing new and
shrewd strikes me at the moment), that I carried in my pocket
a polite, a delicious invitation from Frau Aebi. The invitation
card humbly requested me, and encouraged me, to be so good
as to appear punctually at half past twelve for a modest lunch.
I firmly intended to obey the summons and to emerge promptly
at the time stated in the presence of the estimable person in
question.

Since, dear kind reader, you give yourself the trouble to
march attentively along with the writer and inventor of these
lines, out forthwith into the bright and friendly morning world,
not hurrying, but rather quite at ease, with level head,
smoothly, discreetly, and calmly, now we both arrive in front
of the above-mentioned bakery with the gold inscription,
where we feel inclined to stop, horrified, to stand mournfully
aghast at the gross ostentation and at the sad disfigurement of
sweet rusticity which is intimately connected with it.

Spontaneously I exclaimed: "Pretty indignant, by God,
should any honorable man be, when brought face to face with
such golden inscriptional barbarities, which impress upon the
landscape where we stand the seal of self-seeking, money-grub-
bing, and a miserable, utterly blatant coarsening of the soul.

Does a simple, sincere master baker really require to appear so huge, with his foolish gold and silver proclamations to beam forth and shine, bright as a prince or a dressy, dubious lady? Let him bake and knead his bread in all honor and in reasonable modesty. What sort of a world of swindle are we beginning, or have already begun, to live in, when the municipality, the neighbors, and public opinion not only tolerate but unhappily, it is clear, even applaud that which injures every good sense, every sense of reason and good office, every sense of beauty and probity, that which is morbidly puffed up, offers a ridiculous tawdry show of itself, that which screams out over a hundred yards' distance and more into the good honest air: 'I am such and such. I have so and so much money, and I dare make so bold as to make an unpleasant impression. Of course I am a bumpkin and a blockhead with my hideous ostentation, and a tasteless fellow; but there's nobody can forbid me to be bumpkinish and blockheaded.' Do golden, far-shining, loathsomely glittering letters stand in any acceptable, honorably justified relation, in any healthy affinitive proportion to . . . bread? Not in the least! But loathsome boasting and swaggering began in some corner, in some nook of the world, at some time or other, advanced step by step like a lamentable and disastrous flood, bearing garbage, filth, and foolishness along with them, spreading these throughout the world, and they have affected also my respectable baker, spoiled his earlier good taste, and undermined his inborn decency. I would give much, I would give my left arm, or left leg, if by such a sacrifice I could help recall the fine old sense of sincerity, the old sufficiency, and restore to country and to people the respectability and modesty which have been plentifully lost, to the sorrow of all men who seek honesty. To the devil with every miserable desire to seem more than one is. It is a veritable catastrophe, which spreads over the earth danger of war, death, misery, hate, and injury, and puts upon all that exists an abominable mask of malice and ugliness. I would not have a simple workman a lord, nor a simple woman her ladyship. But everything nowadays is out to dazzle and glitter, to be new and exquisite and beautiful, be lord and lady, and so becomes horrible. But in time perhaps things will change again. I would like to hope so."

Now, as will soon be learned, I shall on account of this haughty bearing, this domineering attitude, take myself to task. In what manner will also soon be shown. It would not be good if I were to criticize others mercilessly, but set about myself only most tenderly and treat myself as indulgently as possible. A critic who goes about it in this way is no true critic, and writers should not practice any abuse of writing. I hope that this sentence pleases all and sundry, inspires satisfaction, and meets with warm applause.

Left of the country road here, a foundry full of workmen and industry causes a noticeable disturbance. In recognition of this I am honestly ashamed to be merely out for a walk while so many others drudge and labor. I drudge away perhaps of course at times, when all these workmen have knocked off and are taking a rest. A fitter on his bicycle, a friend of mine from 135/III Battalion of the militia, calls to me in passing: "It looks to me you're out for a walk again, working hours too!" I wave to him and laugh and blithely admit that he is right, if he thinks I am out for a walk.

"They can all see that I am going for a walk," I thought to myself, and I calmly walked on, without the least annoyance at having been found out, for that would have been silly.

In my bright yellow English suit, which I had received as a present, I really seemed to myself, I must frankly admit, a great lord and grand seigneur, a marquis strolling up and down his park, though it was only a semi-rural, semi-suburban, neat, modest, nice little poor-quarter and country road I walked on, and on no account a noble park, as I have been so arrogant as to suppose, a presumption I gently withdraw, because all that is parklike is pure invention and does not fit here at all. Factories both great and small and mechanical workshops lay scattered agreeably in green countryside. Fat cozy farms meanwhile kindly offered their arms to knocking and hammering industry, which always has something skinny and worn-out about it. Nut trees, cherry trees, and plum trees gave the soft rounded road an attractive, entertaining, and delicate character. A dog lay across the middle of the road which I found as a matter of fact quite beautiful and loved. I loved in fact almost everything I saw as I proceeded, and with a fiery love. Another pretty little dog scene and child scene was as follows. A large but thoroughly comical, humorous, not at all dangerous fellow of a dog was quietly watching a wee scrap of a boy who crouched on some porch steps and bawled on account of the attention which the good-natured yet still somewhat terrifying-looking animal chose to pay him, bawled miserably with fear, setting up a loud and childish wail. I found the scene enchanting; but another childish scene in this country-road theater I found almost more delightful and enchanting. Two very small children were lying on the rather dusty road, as in a garden. One child said to the other: "Now give me a nice little kiss." The other child gave what was so pressingly demanded. Then said the first: "All right, now you may get up." So without a sweet little kiss he would probably never have allowed the other what he now permitted it. "How well this naïve little scene goes with the lovely blue sky, which laughs down so divinely upon the gay, nimble, and bright earth!" I said to myself. "Children are heavenly because they are always in a kind of heaven. When they grow older and grow up, their heaven vanishes and then they fall out of their childishness into the dry calculating manner and tedious perceptions of adults. For the children of poor folk the country road in summer is like a playroom. Where else can they go, seeing that the gardens are selfishly closed to them? Woe to the automobiles blustering by, as they ride coldly and maliciously into the children's games, into the child's heaven, so that small innocent human beings are in danger of being crushed to a pulp. The terrible thought that a child actually can be run over by such a clumsy triumphal car, I dare not think it, otherwise my wrath will seduce me to coarse expressions, with which it is well known nothing much ever gets done."

To people sitting in a blustering dust-churning automobile I always present my austere and angry face, and they do not deserve a better one. Then they believe that I am a spy, a plain-clothes policeman, delegated by high officials and authorities to spy on the traffic, to note down the numbers of vehicles, and later to report them. I always then look darkly at the wheels, at the car as a whole, but never at its occupants, whom I despise, and this in no way personally, but purely on principle; for I do not understand, and I never shall understand, how it can be a pleasure to hurtle past all the images and objects which our beautiful earth displays, as if one had gone mad and had to accelerate for fear of misery and despair. In fact, I love repose and all that reposes. I love thrift and moderation and am in my inmost self, in God's name, unfriendly toward any agitation and haste. More than what is true I need not say. And because of these words the driving of automobiles will certainly not be discontinued, nor its evil air-polluting smell, which nobody for sure particularly loves or esteems. It would be unnatural if someone's nostrils were to love and inhale with relish that which for all correct nostrils, at times, depending perhaps on the mood one is in, outrages and evokes revulsion. Enough, and no harm meant. And now walk on. Oh, it is heavenly and good and in simplicity most ancient to walk on foot, provided of course one's shoes or boots are in order.

Would the esteemed ladies and gentlemen, patrons and patronesses and circles of readers, while they benevolently tolerate and condone this perhaps somewhat too solemn and high-strutting style, now be so kind as to allow me duly to draw their attention to two particularly significant persons, forms, or figures, namely firstly, or better, first, to an alleged retired actress, and secondly to the most youthful presumed budding cantatrice? I hold these two people to be considerably weighty and therefore I believed it wise to announce and advertise them properly in advance, before they enter and figure in reality, so that an odor of significance and fame may run before these two gentle creatures, and they may be received and observed on their appearance with all distinction, due regard, and loving concern, such as one should, in my diminutive opinion, almost compulsorily accord to such beings. Then at about half past twelve the writer will, as is known, in reward for his many labors, eat, carouse, and dine in the palazzo, or house, of Frau Aebi. Till then, however, he will have to cover a considerable stretch of his road, and write a fair quantity of lines. But one realizes to be sure to satiety that he loves to walk as well as he loves to write; the latter of course perhaps just a shade less than the former.

In front of a very attractive house I saw, very close to the beautiful road, a woman seated on a bench, and hardly had I glimpsed her when I plucked up the courage to speak, addressing her, in the most polite and courteous terms possible, as follows:

"Forgive me, a person utterly unknown to you, if at the sight of you the eager and assuredly saucy question forces itself to my lips, whether you have not perhaps been formerly an actress? For in fact you seem very much indeed like a once great, indulged, celebrated actress and stage artist. Certainly you quite rightly wonder at my so amazingly rash address and obstreperous inquiry; but you have such a beautiful face, such a pleasant, charming, and, I must add, interesting appearance, present such a beautiful, noble, fine aspect, look so candidly, majestically, and calmly out of your eyes upon me and upon the world in general, that I could not possibly have compelled myself to pass you by without daring to say something civil and flattering to you, which I hope you will not hold against me, although I am afraid that I deserve correction and admonishment on account of my frivolity. When I saw you I thought for a moment that you must have been an actress, and today, I mused, you sit here beside the simple, though at the same time beautiful, road, in front of the pretty little shop, whose owner you appear to me to be. You have perhaps before today never been so unceremoniously addressed. Your friendly and moreover graceful aspect, your hospitable, beautiful appearance, your equanimity, your fine figure, and this noble, cheerful air in your advancing years (this I trust you will allow me to observe) have encouraged me to engage with you in intimate conversation on the open road. This fine day also, delighting me as it does with its freedom and gaiety, has kindled in me a joyousness, in consequence of which I have perhaps gone too far with the unknown lady. You smile! Then you are in no way angered by the unconstrained quality of my utterance. I think it, if I may say so, well and good when from time to time two persons who are unacquainted freely and harmlessly converse, for which converse we inhabitants of this wandering curious planet, which is a puzzle to us, do, when all is said and done, possess mouth and tongue and linguistic capacity, which last is as a matter of fact both curious and fair. In any case, the moment I saw you, I liked you profoundly; but now I must reverently ask your pardon, and I would ask you to rest assured that you inspire me with the warmest feelings of respect. Can this full confession that I was very glad when I saw you cause you to be angry with me?"

"It is far rather a pleasure for me," said the beautiful woman happily. "But, in reference to your supposition, I must prepare you for a disappointment. I have never been an actress."

At this I felt moved to say: "Not long ago I came into this region out of cold, forlorn, and narrow circumstances, inwardly sick, completely without faith, without confidence or trust, without any finer sort of hope, a stranger to the world and to myself, and hostile to both. Timidity and mistrust took me prisoner and accompanied my every step. Then, little by little, I lost my ignoble, ugly prejudices. Here I breathed again more quiet and free—and became again a better, warmer, and happier man. The terrors which filled my soul I saw gradually vanish; misery and emptiness in my heart and my hopefulness were slowly transformed into gay content and into a pleasant, lively sympathy, which I learned to feel anew. I was dead, and now it is as if someone had raised me up and set me on my way. Where I thought I must meet with much that is repulsive, hard, and disquieting, I encounter charm and goodness, I find all that is docile, familiar, and good."

"So much the better," said the woman, and her face and voice were kind.

As the moment seemed to have come to conclude this conversation, somewhat truculently begun, and to withdraw, I presented my compliments to the woman whom I had taken for an actress, but who was now unfortunately a great and famous actress no longer, as she herself had found it necessary to protest, with, I should add, an exquisite and very scrupulous courtesy, bowed to her and quietly, as if nothing had ever happened, walked on my way.

A modest question: An elegant milliner's under green trees, does this perhaps by now arouse exceptional interest and evoke possibly a little if any applause?

I firmly believe it does, and so I dare to communicate the most humble observation, that as I walked and marched along on the most beautiful of roads a somewhat foolish, juvenile, and loud shout of joy burst from my throat, a throat which did not itself consider this, or anything like it, possible. What did I see and discover that was new, astounding, and beautiful? Oh, quite simply the above-mentioned milliner's and fashion salon. Paris and St. Petersburg, Bucharest and Milan, London and Berlin, all that is elegant, naughty, and metropolitan, drew close to me, emerged before me, to fascinate and to enchant me. But in the capitals of the world one misses the green and luscious embellishments of trees, the embellishment and beneficence of friendly fields and many delicate little leaves and, last but not least, the sweet fragrance of flowers, and this I had here. "All this," so I proposed to myself as I stood there, "I shall certainly soon write down in a piece or sort of fantasy, which I shall entitle "The Walk." Especially this ladies' hat shop may not be omitted. Otherwise, a most picturesque charm would be missing from the piece, and this lack I shall know as well to avoid as to circumvent and render impossible." The feathers, ribbons, artificial fruits and flowers on the nice quaint hats were to me almost as attractive and homely as nature herself, who, with her natural green, with her natural colors, framed and so delicately enclosed the artificial colors and fantastic shapes of fashion that the milliner's might have been simply a delightful painting. I rely here, as I said, on the most subtle understanding of the reader, of whom I am honestly afraid. This miserable and cowardly confession is understandable. It is the same with all the more courageous authors.

God! what did I see, likewise under leaves, but a bewitching, dainty, delightful butcher shop, with rose-red pork, beef, and lamb displayed. The butcher was bustling about inside, where his customers stood also. This butcher shop is certainly as well worth a shout as the shop with the hats. Third, a grocer's might merit a quiet mention. To all sorts of public houses I come later, which is, I think, quite soon enough. With public houses, doubtless one cannot begin late enough in the day, because they produce consequences which everybody knows, knows indeed to satiety. Even the most virtuous person cannot dispute the fact that he is never master of certain improprieties. Luckily, however, one is of course—human, and as such easily pardonable. One simply appeals to the weakness of the system.

Here once again I must take fresh bearings. I assume that I can effect the reorganization and regrouping of forces as well as any field marshal surveying all circumstances and drawing all contingencies and reverses into the net of his, it will be permitted me to say, genius for computation. In the daily papers at present an industrious person can read such things every day, and he notes such expressions as "flank attack." I have recently come to the conclusion that the art and direction of war is almost as difficult, and requires almost as much patience, as the art of writing, the converse being also true. Writers also, like generals, often make the most laborious preparations before they dare march to the attack and give battle, or, in other words, fling their produce, or a book, into the book market, an action which serves as a challenge and thus vigorously stimulates very forceful counterattacks. Books attract discussions, and these sometimes end in such a fury that the book must die and its writer despair of it all.

I hope no estrangement will ensue if I say that I am writing all these I trust pretty and delicate lines with a quill from the Imperial High Court of Justice. Hence the brevity, pregnancy, and acumen of my language, at certain points well enough perceptible, at which now nobody need wonder any more.

But when shall I come at last to the well-earned banquet with my Frau Aebi? I fear it will take quite a time, as considerable obstacles must first be put aside. Appetite in unstinted abundance has been long enough present.

As I went on my way, like a better sort of tramp, a vagabond and pickpocket, or idler and vagrant of a sort finer than some, past all sorts of gardens planted and stuffed full with placid, contented vegetables, past flowers and fragrance of flowers, past fruit trees and past beansticks and shrubs full of beans, past towering crops, as rye, barley, and wheat, past a woodyard containing much wood and wood shavings, past juicy grass and past a gently splashing little waterway, rivulet, or stream, past all sorts of people, as choice trade-plying market women, tripping past, and past a clubhouse decoratively hung with banners flying for a celebration, or for joy, and also past many other good-hearted and useful things, past a particularly beautiful and sweet little fairy apple tree, and past God knows what else in the way of feasible things, as, for example, also strawberry bushes and blossoms, or, even better, gracefully past the ripe red strawberries, while all sorts of more or less beautiful and pleasant thoughts continued to preoccupy me, since, when I'm out walking, many notions, flashes of light, and lightning flashes quite of their own accord intrude and interrupt, to be carefully pondered upon, there came a man in my direction, an enormity, a monster, who almost completely darkened my bright and shining road, a tall, lanky beanpole of a fellow, sinister, whom I knew alas only too well, a very curious customer; namely the giant

TOMZACK

In any other place and on any other road but this dear yielding country road I would have expected him. His woeful, gruesome air, his tragic, atrocious appearance, infused me with terror and took every good, bright, and beautiful prospect, all

joy and gaiety away from me. Tomzack! It is true, dear reader,
is it not, the name alone has the sound of terrible and mournful
things? "Why do you persecute me, why need you meet me
here in the middle of my road, you miserable creature?" I cried
to him; but Tomzack gave me no answer. He turned his great
eyes upon me; that is, he looked down from high up on me
below; for he surpassed me in length and height by very considerable degrees. Beside him, I felt like a dwarf, or like a poor
weak little child. With the greatest of ease the giant could have
trodden me underfoot and crushed me. Oh, I knew who he
was. For him there was no rest. Restlessly he went up and
down in the world. He slept in no soft bed, and could live in no
comfortable homely house. He was at home everywhere and
nowhere. He had no home country, and of no state was he a
citizen. Without motherland and without happiness he was;
he had to live completely without love and without human joy.
He had sympathy with no man, and with him and his mopping
and mowing no man had sympathy. Past, present, and future
were to him an insubstantial desert, and life was too small, too
tiny, too narrow for him. For him there was nothing which had
meaning, and he himself in turn meant something to nobody.
Out of his great eyes there broke a glare of grief in overworlds
and underworlds. Infinite pain spoke from his slack and weary
moments. A hundred thousand years old he seemed to me, and
it seemed to me that he must live for eternity, only to be for
eternity no living being. He died every instant and yet he could
not die. For him there was no grave with flowers on it. I eluded
him, and murmured to myself: "Goodbye, keep well nevertheless, friend Tomzack!"

Without looking back at the phantom, the pitiful colossus
and superman, and candidly I had not the remotest desire to do
so, I walked on and soon afterwards, proceeding thus in the
warm yielding air and erasing the sad impression which the
strange figure of a man, or rather of a giant, had made upon
me, I came into a pine forest, through which coiled a smiling,
serpentine, and at the same time roguishly graceful path,
which I followed with pleasure. Path and forest floor were as

a carpet, and here within the forest it was quiet as in a happy human soul, as in the interior of a temple, as in a palace and enchanted dream-wrapped fairy-tale castle, as in Sleeping Beauty's castle, where all sleep, and all are hushed for centuries of long years. I penetrated deeper, and I speak perhaps a little indulgently if I say that to myself I seemed like a prince with golden hair, his body clad in warrior's armor. So solemn was it in the forest that lovely and solemn imaginings, quite of their own accord, took possession of the sensitive walker there. How glad I was at this sweet forest softness and repose! From time to time, from outside, a slight sound or two penetrated the delicious seclusion and bewitching darkness, perhaps a bang, a whistle, or some other noise, whose distant note would only intensify the prevailing soundlessness, which I inhaled to my very heart's content, and whose virtues I drank and quaffed with due ceremony. Here and there in all this tranquillity and quietude a bird let his blithe voice be heard out of his charmed and holy hiding place. Thus I stood and listened, and suddenly there came upon me an inexpressible feeling for the world, and, together with it, a feeling of gratitude, which broke powerfully out of my soul. The pines stood straight as pillars there, and not the least thing moved in the whole delicate forest, throughout which all kinds of inaudible voices seemed to echo and sound. Music out of the primeval world, from whence I cannot tell, stole on my ear. "Oh, thus, if it must be, shall I then willingly end and die. A memory will then delight me even in the grave, and a gratitude enliven me even in death; a thanksgiving for the pleasures, for the joys, for the ecstasies; a thanksgiving for life, and a joy at joy." High up, a gentle rustling, whispering down from the treetops, could be heard. "To love and to kiss here must be divinely beautiful," I told myself. Simply to tread on the pleasant ground became a joy, and the stillness kindled prayers in the feeling soul. "To be dead here, and to lie inconspicuous in the cool forest earth must be sweet. Oh, that one could sense and enjoy death even in death! Perhaps one can. To have a small, quiet grave in the forest would be lovely. Perhaps I should hear the singing of the birds and

the forest rustling above me. I would like that." Marvelous
between trunks of oaks a pillar of sunbeams fell into the forest,
which to me seemed like a delicious green grave. Soon I
stepped out into the radiant open again, and into life.

Now there should come, as it emerges here, an inn, and,
that is, a very fine, attractive, and coaxing one, an inn situated
near the edge of the forest out of which I have this moment
walked, an inn with a charming garden full of refreshing shade.
The garden should lie on a pretty hill with a good view all
around, and right beside it there should stand an extra, artificial hill, or bastion, where one could stay and for quite a long
time enjoy the splendid prospect. A glass of beer or wine would
also certainly not be unwelcome; but the person who is out
walking here recalls just in time that his excursion is not really
all that strenuous. The toilsome mountains lie far off in the
bluish, luminous, white-misted distance. He must frankly confess that his thirst is neither murderous nor heathenish, since
till now he has had to cover only relatively short stretches of
the road. Indeed, it is here a question more of a delicate, gentle
walk than of a voyage or excursion, more of a subtle circular
stroll than a forced march; and therefore he justly, as well as
wisely, declines to enter the house of joy and refreshment, and
he takes his leave. All serious people who read this will certainly accord him affluent applause for his fine decision and
goodwill. Did I not, as much as an hour ago, take the opportunity of announcing a young songstress? Now she enters.

Enters, that is, at a ground-level window.

For now I returned from the forest recess to the highway,
and there I heard——

But stop! Relax in brief respite. Writers who understand
their profession take the same as easily as possible. From time
to time they like to lay their pens aside a while. Uninterrupted
writing fatigues, like digging.

What I heard from the ground-level window was the most
delicious, fresh folk or opera song, a matutinal banquet of
sound, a morning concert, which entered my astonished ears
completely free of charge. A young girl, still a schoolgirl, but

slim already and tall, was standing in her bright dress at a drab suburban window, and this girl was singing out and up into the blue air simply ecstatically. Most agreeably surprised, and enchanted by the unexpected song, I stood a little to the side lest I might disturb the singer and rob myself both of my attendance and of my pleasure. The song which the little one sang seemed to be of a cheerful and delicious nature; the notes had the very sound itself of young innocent joy in life and in love; they flew, like angel figures wearing the snow-white plumage of delight, up into the heavens, whence they seemed to fall down again and to die smiling. It was like dying from affliction, dying perhaps also from too delicate a delight, like a too exultant loving and living and a powerlessness to live any more because of a too rich and beautiful vision of life, so that to some extent its tender thought, overflowing with joy and love, rushing exuberantly into being, seemed to fall over itself and break itself in pieces. When the girl has finished her simple but rich and charming song, her melodious Mozartian or shepherd girl's aria, I went up to her, greeted her, asked her for permission to congratulate her on her beautiful voice, and complimented her on her extraordinarily spiritual performance. The little songstress, who looked like a doe, or a sort of antelope in girl's form, looked at me with her beautiful brown eyes full of question and surprise. She had a very delicate, gentle face, and she gave me a captivating and polite smile. "To you," I said to her, "if you know how to train carefully and tend your beautiful, young, and rich voice, a process which will require your own intelligence as well as that of others, belongs a brilliant future and a great career; for to me you seem, I frankly and honestly confess, to be the great operatic singer of the future in person! You are obviously clever, you are tender and supple, and you possess, if my suppositions do not entirely deceive me, a most decidedly courageous soul. You have fire, and an evident nobility of heart; this I just heard in the song which you sang so beautifully and really well. You have talent, but more: you have indubitably genius! And now I speak no vain and untrue words. I take it upon myself therefore to ask you to pay very special attention to your noble gift, to preserve it from deformity, mutilation, and thoughtless premature exhaustion. At present, I can only tell you in all sincerity that you sing exceedingly well, and that this is something very serious; for it means much; it means above all that you will be expected industriously to sing a little bit further every day. Practice and sing with wise, beautiful moderation. The extent and scope of the treasure in your possession you yourself certainly know not at all. In your vocal accomplishment there sounds already a high degree of natural grace, a rich sum of unsuspecting vigorous being and life, and an abundance of poetry and humanity. It is permissible to tell you, and to give you positive assurance, that you therefore promise to become in every way a genuine singer, because it is likely that you are a person who is compelled to sing by her very inmost nature, and who appears only to live, and only to be able to enjoy life, when she begins to sing, thus transforming all her actual delight in life into the art of song, whence all that is humanly and personally significant, all that is suffused with soul, all that is full of understanding, ascends into something higher, into an ideal. In a beautiful song there is always a concentration and compression of experience, perception, and feeling, an explosive aggregate of condensed life and animation of the soul, and with such a song, a woman who makes good use of her situation, and mounts the ladder of her opportunities, may as a star in the firmament of music move profoundly the hearts of many people, amass great wealth, transport a public to demonstrations of stormy and enthusiastic applause, and draw down upon herself the sincere love and admiration of kings and of queens."

Serious, and astonished, the girl listened to the words I spoke, though I uttered them certainly more for my own delight than in any hope that the little thing might appreciate and understand them, for she lacked the necessary maturity.

From afar I can already see a railway crossing which I shall have to traverse; but, at present, I have not got that far; for I shall have, it must be clearly realized, two or three important commissions to execute, and several insuperable arrangements to make. On these commissions a report must be drawn up, or delivered, in as much detail, and with as much precision, as possible. It will generously be permitted me to remark that I have in passing to present myself with all expediency at an elegant gentleman's outfitters or tailor's workshop to discuss a new suit which I must try on and have tailored. Second, I have to pay off heavy taxes in the local office or town hall; and third, I ought to take a noteworthy letter to the post office and throw it into the letter box. It will be seen how much I have to do, and how this apparently idle and easygoing walk is full of practical business affairs, and people will therefore, I hope, be so good as to excuse my loitering, appreciate my delays, and approve the long-winded discussions with professional and clerical people; yes, perhaps even welcome them as acceptable adjuncts and contributions to the entertainment. For all consequent lengths, breadths, and heights I humbly request in advance the reader's pardon. Has a provincial or metropolitan author ever been more diffident and courteous toward the circle of his readers? I hardly think so, and therefore, with my conscience utterly clear, I continue my little chat and narrative and report the following:

God bless my soul! It's high time I went over to Frau Aebi for my dinner, or lunch. This very minute it is striking half past twelve. As luck would have it, the lady lives very near indeed to where I am standing; I need only slip, smooth as an eel, into the house, as into a loophole, and as into a shelter for poor starvelings and pitiful distressed gentlefolk.

FRAU AEBI

received me most magnanimously. My punctuality was a masterpiece. It is known how rare masterpieces are. Frau Aebi smiled when she saw me arriving, really most kindly. She offered me, in a cordial and winning way, which in a manner of speaking enchanted me, her nice little hand, and led me at once into the dining room, where she requested me to sit at the table, a request which I naturally and with the utmost conceivable pleasure, and completely without restraint, fulfilled. Without making the least ridiculous fuss, I began harmlessly and without reserve to eat and stoutly help myself, and I was a long way from guessing what was in store for me. Anyway, I began boldly to help myself and stoutly to eat. Such boldness, as is well known, costs not much in the way of sacrifice. With some surprise, however, I observed that Frau Aebi was watching me with something like devotion. This was quite noticeable. Obviously, it moved her deeply to watch how I helped myself and ate. This curious situation astonished me, but I attributed no major significance to it. The moment I wanted to supply a little conversation and diversion, Frau Aebi stopped me and said that she declined all forms of diversion with the greatest pleasure. This curious phrase took me aback, and I began to be anxious and afraid. Quite secretly I began to be terrified in Frau Aebi's presence. When I wanted to stop cutting it up and popping it in, because I distinctly felt that I was full, she said to me in an almost delicate manner and tone of voice, through which gently shuddered a maternal rebuke: "But you are not eating! Wait, I'll cut you another big juicy slice." A sense of dread rippled through me, and I plucked up the courage to object, politely and courteously, that my main purpose in coming here had been to deploy a certain intellectuality, whereupon Frau Aebi, smiling most captivatingly, said that she did not think this to be at all necessary. "I cannot possibly go on eating," I said, in a dull muffled voice. I was almost suffocating, and was already perspiring with terror. Frau Aebi said: "I cannot possibly believe that you want to stop cutting it up and popping it in, and I do not think that you are really full at all. Quite definitely you are not telling the truth when you say that you are just about suffocating. I am compelled to consider that as mere politeness. I decline any form of intellectual chat, as I have already said, with pleasure. Certainly your main purpose in coming to me was to prove and demonstrate that you have a good appetite and are a big eater. This consideration I cannot under any circumstances forego. I would cordially ask you to be sensible and accommodate yourself to the inevitable; for I can assure you that there is no possibility that you will leave this table before you have eaten up and polished off everything that I have cut, and will cut, off for you. I am afraid you are helplessly vanquished; for you must realize that there are housewives who compel their guests to help themselves and pack themselves to the brim, until they burst. A deplorable, lamentable fate awaits you; but you must endure it bravely. Each of us in due course has to make some great sacrifice. So obey and eat. For to obey surely is sweet. What harm is done, if you perish in the attempt? Here, this most delicate, delicious, and large slice you must certainly demolish, I know you will. Courage, my good friend! We all need to be brave. What worth are we, if we persist forever steadfast in our own will? Concentrate all your strenth, and compel yourself to do the loftiest deed, to endure the most difficult trial, and to survive the most arduous struggle. You cannot believe how glad I am to watch you eat till you drop unconscious. You cannot imagine how disappointed I would be if you were to refuse me this; but you will do it, won't you? You'll bite your best and help yourself, won't you, even if you are so full that your back teeth are floating?"

"Terrible woman! What do you want with me?" I exclaimed and sprang up from the table and made as if to rush out and away. Frau Aebi, however, held me back, laughed aloud and cordially, and confessed that she had permitted herself a joke with me, which I would please be so good as not to grudge her. "I only wanted to give you an example of how it is done by certain housewives, who almost overflow with kindness toward their guests."

At this I had to laugh to myself, and I may admit that in her exuberance I liked Frau Aebi very much. She wanted to have me near her the whole afternoon, and was almost a little indignant when I told her that it was, unfortunately for me, an impossible thing for me to afford her my company any longer, because I had to settle certain important affairs, which I could not put off. It was extremely flattering to me to hear Frau Aebi so vigorously regretting that I had to leave again so soon and wanted to. She asked me if it was really so pressingly urgent to abscond and vanish, whereupon I gave her the most holy assurances that only the most pressing urgencies had the ability and power to draw me away so soon from such a pleasant house and from such an attractive, esteemed person, with which words I look my leave of her.

It was now meet to conquer, master, surprise, and abash in his unshakable convictions an obstinate, recalcitrant tailor, or *marchand tailleur*, a person obviously in every respect convinced of the infallibility of his doubtless eminent skill, and completely saturated with a sense of his own efficiency. The crippling of a master tailor's fixity of mind must be considered one of the most difficult and hazardous tasks which courage can undertake and daredevil determination determine to carry forward. Of tailors and their opinions I have a comprehensive, constant, and intense fear; I am not at all ashamed of this sad admission; for fear is, in this instance, explicable and understandable. I was, then, prepared for trouble, perhaps even for trouble of the worst and most terrible kind, and I armed myself for this highly perilous attack with qualities such as courage, scorn, wrath, indignation, disdain, even the disdain of death; and with these indubitably very appreciable weapons I hoped to advance, successfully and victoriously, against biting irony and mockery lurking under a simulation of friendliness. It turned out otherwise; but I will be silent on this point till later, particularly as first I still have to dispatch a letter. For I have just decided to go first to the post office, then to the tailor, and only after this to pay my taxes. Besides, the post office, a tasteful building, lay right in front of my nose; and I blithely went in and besought the responsible post office official for a stamp, which I stuck upon the envelope. While I then circumspectly slipped the same down into the letter box, I examined and weighed pensively, in my mind, what I had written. As I very well knew, the contents were as follows:

Most respectable Sir,

The curious form of address should bring you the assurance that the writer confronts you quite coldly. I know that respect of myself is not to be expected from you, nor from any persons of your sort; for you and persons of your sort have an exorbitant opinion of themselves, which hinders them from achieving understanding and discretion. I know with certainty that you are one of those people who seem to themselves important because they are inconsiderate and discourteous, who think themselves powerful because they enjoy protection, and believe themselves wise because the little word "wise" happens to occur to them. People like you are so bold as to be hard, impudent, coarse, and violent with regard to people who are poor and unprotected. People like you possess the extraordinary wit to believe that it is necessary to be everywhere on top, to keep everywhere the ascendancy, and to triumph at every moment of the day. People like you do not observe that this is foolish, that it neither lies within the bounds of possibility nor is in any way to be desired. People like you are snobs and are ready at all times industriously to serve brutality. People like you are exceedingly courageous in the evasion of any sort of genuine courage, because they know that this true courage promises to injure them; and they are courageous in demonstrating with an uncommon degree of pleasure and an uncommon degree of zeal their right to set up as the good and the beautiful. People like you respect neither old age nor merit, and certainly not hard work. People like you respect money, and your respect of money obstructs any higher estimation of other things. He who works honestly, and diligently exerts himself, is in the eyes of people like you an outspoken ass. I do not err; for my little finger can tell me that I am right. I dare tell you to your face that you abuse your position because you know full well how many complications and annoyances would be entailed if anyone were to rap your knuckles; but in the grace and favor which you enjoy, ensconced in your privileged prescriptive position, you are still wide open to attack; for you feel without a doubt how insecure you are. You betray confidence, do not keep your word, injure without a second thought the virtues and reputations of those who have to deal with you; you rob unsparingly where you pretend to institute beneficence, impose upon the services and denigrate the person of every willing servant, you are exceedingly fickle and unreliable, and show qualities which one might willingly pardon in a girl, but not in a man. Forgive me that I should have allowed myself to think you very weak, and accept, with the candid assurance that I consider it advisable to avoid any future contact with you in my affairs, the required measure and the established degree of respect from a person upon whom devolved the distinction and inevitably moderate pleasure of having made your acquaintance.

I almost regretted now that I had entrusted to the post for dispatch and delivery this cutthroat's letter, for as such it now subsequently appeared to me: indeed, to no less than a leading, influential personality I had in such an ideal manner proclaimed, thus conjuring up a furious state of war, the rupture of diplomatic or, better, economic relations. Still, I unleashed my challenge, while I consoled myself with the reflection that this personality, or most respectable sir, would perhaps never even read my communication, because, on perusing and relishing even the second or third word of it, he would probably have had quite enough, and he would presumably hurl the blazing effusion, without losing much time or energy about it, into his all-devouring, all-accommodating wastepaper basket. "Besides, in the course of nature, a thing like this is forgotten in six or three months," I concluded and philosophized and marched, *bravement*, to my tailor.

The same sat happily, and with what seemed the clearest conscience in the world, in his elegant fashion salon or workshop, which was stuffed and crammed with subtly fragrant rolls and remnants of cloth. In an aviary, or cage, blustered, to complete the idyllic scene, a bird, and a keen crafty apprentice was nicely occupied with cutting out. Herr Dünn the master tailor rose as he caught sight of me most courteously from his seat, upon which he had been diligently fencing with his needle, to bid the visitor a friendly welcome. "You have come about your suit, an unquestionably impeccable fit, which is soon to be delivered complete and finished by my firm," he said, as he tendered me, perhaps a little too companionably, his hand, which I nevertheless was not in the least hesitant vigorously to shake. "I have come," I parried, "to proceed dauntlessly and full of hope to the fitting, though I have my fears."

Herr Dünn said that he considered all my fears to be superfluous and that he guaranteed both the fit and the cut, and, as he was saying this, he accompanied me into an adjoining room, from which he himself at once withdrew. He guaranteed and protested repeatedly, and this did not really quite please me. The fitting, and the disappointment which was so intimately connected with it, was soon complete. I shouted, attempting meanwhile to fight back an overflowing chargin, loudly and energetically for Herr Dünn, at whom, with the greatest possible composure and genteel dissatisfaction, I flung the annihilating outburst: "It's exactly as I thought!"

"My dear and most esteemed sir, it is useless to excite yourself!"

Laboriously enough I brought out: "Here's cause enough and plenty to spare that I should get excited and be inconsolable. Keep your highly inept attempts at appeasement to yourself and be so kind as to upset me no longer; for what you have done in the way of making a faultless suit is in the highest degree upsetting. All the delicate or indelicate fears that arose in me have been justfied, and my worst expectations have been fulfilled. How can you dare to guarantee a faultless cut and fit, and how is it possible that you have the audacity to assure me that you are a master in your craft, when you must confess, even with only a very sparse measure of honesty and with only the smallest degree of honorable dealing and perceptiveness, that I am entirely displeased and that the faultless suit to be delivered to me by your esteemed and excellent firm is completely botched?"

"I must courteously disallow the term 'botched'."

"I will control my feelings, Herr Dünn."

"I thank you and am cordially delighted by this most pleasant resolve."

"You will allow me to expect of you that you make considerable alterations to this suit, which, as evidenced by the recent fitting, reveals multitudes of mistakes, defects, and blemishes."

"I might."

"The dissatisfaction, the displeasure, and the grief I feel, force me to inform you that you have vexed me."

"I swear to you that I am sorry."

"The assiduity with which you choose to swear that you are sorry to have vexed me and put me in the worst possible humor does not in the least modify the defectiveness of the suit, to which I refuse to accord even the smallest degree of recognition, and acceptance of which I vigorously reject, since there can be no question of any approbation and applause. As regards the jacket, I clearly feel that it makes me a hunchback, and therefore hideous, a deformation with which I can under no circumstances admit myself to concur. On the contrary, I do really feel obliged to protest against such a wicked extravagance and addition to my body. The sleeves suffer from an objectionable surfeit of length, and the waistcoat is eminently distinguished in that it creates the impression and evokes the unpleasant semblance of my being the bearer of a fat stomach. The trousers, or trouserings, are absolutely disgusting. The design and scheme of these trousers inspire me with a genuine feeling of horror. Where this miserable, idiotic, and ridiculous work of trouserly art should possess a certain width, it exhibits a very straitlaced narrowness, and where it should be narrow, it is more than wide. Your execution, Herr Dünn, is in sum unimaginative, and your work manifests an absence of intelligence. There adheres to this suit something despicable, something petty-minded, something inane, something homemade, something ridiculous, and something fearful. The man who made it can certainly not be counted among men of spirit. Regrettable indeed is such an absolute absence of talent."

Herr Dünn had the imperturbability to reply: "I do not understand your indignation, nor shall I ever be persuaded to understand you. The numerous violent reproofs which you feel obliged to heap upon me are incomprehensible to me, and will very probably remain incomprehensible. The suit fits you very well. Nobody can make me think otherwise. My conviction that you appear uncommonly to your advantage in it, I declare to be unshakable. To certain distinguishing features and peculiarities of it you will soon become accustomed. Very high-up state officials order their estimable requirements from me; graciously likewise do Justices of the Peace send me their commissions. This assuredly striking proof of my capability should satisfy you. For exaggerated expectations and imaginings I cannot cater, and master tailor Dünn does not admit any arrogant demands. Better situated persons and more eminent gentlemen than you have been in every respect satisfied with my proficiency and skill. The insinuation of my claim should disarm you."

Since I had to agree that it was impossible to accomplish anything, and since I had to consider that my perhaps excessively fiery and impetuous onslaught had been transformed into a painful and ignominious defeat, I withdrew my troops from this unfortunate engagement, broke feebly off, and flew the field in shame. In such manner was concluded the audacious adventure with the tailor. Without another glance about me, I sped to the municipal treasury, or revenue office, to settle my taxes; but here I must correct a gross error.

It was, that is to say, a question not of payment, as it now subsequently occurs to me, but merely, for the time being, of a personal discussion with the President of the laudable Commission for Revenues, and of the handing in, or handing over, of a solemn declaration. May my readers not hold this error against me, but listen generously to what I have to say in this connection. As adequately as the resolute and unshakable master tailor Dünn promised and guaranteed faultlessness, so do I promise and guarantee, with regard to the declaration to be rendered, exactitude and completeness, as well as concision and brevity.

With a bound I enter the charming situation in question. "Permit me to inform you," I said frankly and freely to the tax man—or high revenue official—who gave me his governmental ear in order to follow with appropriate attentiveness the report I was about to deliver, "that I enjoy, as a poor writer and pen-pusher or *homme de lettres*, a very dubious income. Naturally you will not see or find in my case the smallest trace of an amassed fortune. I affirm this with deep regret, without, however, despair or any tears over the lamentable fact. I get along as best I can, as they say. I dispense with all luxuries: this, a single glance at my person should tell you. The food I eat can be described as sufficient and frugal. It occurred to you to consider that I might be lord and master of many sources of income; but I am compelled to oppose, courteously but decisively, this belief and all such suppositions, and to tell the simple unadorned truth, and this truth is that I am extremely free from wealth, but, on the other hand, laden with every sort of poverty, as you might be so kind as to write in your notebook. On Sundays I may not allow myself to be seen on the streets, for I have no Sunday clothes. In my steady and thrifty way of life I am like a field mouse. A sparrow has better prospects of prosperity than this deliverer of a report and taxpayer you see before you. I have written books, which the public unfortunately does not like, and the consequences of this oppress my heart. I do not for a moment doubt that you understand this, and that you consequently realize my financial situation. Ordinary civil status and civil esteem I do not possess; that's as clear as daylight. There seems to be no sense of obligation toward men such as myself. Exceedingly few persons profess a lively interest in literature, and the pitiless criticism of our work, which any manjack assumes he can practice and foster, constitutes yet another abundant source of hurt, and, like a drag chain, drags down the aspirant accomplisher of a state of modest well-being. Of course there exist amicable patrons and friendly patronesses, who subsidize me most nobly from time to time; but a gift is no income, and a subsidy is no fortune. For all these self-explanatory and I hope convincing reasons, most honoured sir, I would request you to overlook all the increases in taxation which you have communicated to me, and I must ask, if not implore you, in my case to set your rate of taxation at as low a level as possible."

The superintendent or inspector of taxes said: "But you're always to be seen out for a walk!"

"Walk," was my answer, "I definitely must, to invigorate myself and to maintain contact with the living world, without perceiving which I could not write the half of one more single word, or produce the tiniest poem in verse or prose. Without walking, I would be dead, and my profession, which I love passionately, would be destroyed. Also, without walking and gathering reports, I would not be able to render one single further report, or the tiniest of essays, let alone a real, long story. Without walking, I would not be able to make any observations or any studies at all. Such a clever and enlightened man as you may and will understand this at once. On a lovely and far-wandering walk a thousand usable and useful thoughts occur to me. Shut in at home, I would miserably decay and dry up. Walking is for me not only healthy and lovely, it is also of service and useful. A walk advances me professionally and provides me at the same time also with amusement and joy; it refreshes and comforts and delights me, is a pleasure for me, and simultaneously, it has the peculiarity that it allures me and spurs me on to further creation, since it offers me as material numerous small and large objectivities upon which I later work at home, diligently and industriously. A walk is always filled with significant phenomena, which are valuable to see and to feel. A pleasant walk most often teems with imageries and living poems, with enchantments and natural beauties, be they ever so small. The lore of nature and the lore of the country are revealed, charming and graceful, to the sense and eyes of the observant walker, who must of course walk not with downcast but with open and unclouded eyes, if the lovely significance and the gay, noble idea of the walk are to dawn on him. Consider how the poet must grow impoverished and run sadly to ruin if that maternal and paternal and, in beauty childlike, beautiful nature does not ever and again refresh him from the source of the good and of the beautiful. Consider the great unabating importance for the poet of the instruction and golden holy teaching which he derives out there in the play of the open air. Without walking and the contemplation of nature which is connected with it, without this equally delicious and admonishing search, I deem myself lost, and I am lost. With the utmost love and attention the man who walks must study and observe every smallest living thing, be it a child, a dog, a fly, a butterfly, a sparrow, a worm, a flower, a man, a house, a tree, a hedge, a snail, a mouse, a cloud, a hill, a leaf, or no more than a poor discarded scrap of paper on which, perhaps, a dear good child at school has written his first clumsy letters. The highest and the lowest, the most serious and the most hilarious things are to him equally beloved, beautiful, and valuable. He must bring with him no sort of sentimentally sensitive self-love or quickness to take offense. Unselfish and unegoistic, he must let his careful eye wander and stroll where it will; only he must be continuously able in the contemplation and observation of things to efface himself, and to put behind him, little consider, and forget like a brave, zealous, and joyfully self-immolating front-line soldier, himself, his private complaints, needs, wants, and sacrifices. If he does not, then he walks only half attentive, with only half his spirit, and that is worth nothing. He must at all times be capable of compassion, of sympathy, and of enthusiasm, and it is hoped that he is. He must be able to bow down and sink into the deepest and smallest everyday thing, and it is probable that he can. Faithful, devoted self-effacement and self-surrender among objects, and zealous love for all phenomena and things, make him happy in this, however, just as every performance of duty make that man happy and rich in his inmost being who is aware of his duty. Spirit, devotion, and faithfulness bless him and raise him high up above his own inconspicuous walking self, which has only too often a name and evil reputation for vagabondage and vagrancy. His manifold studies enrich and hearten, appease and ennoble him, and moreover, however improbable it may sound, they touch the fringes of exact science, a thing of which nobody would think the apparently frivolous wanderer capable. Do you realize that I am working obstinately and tenaciously with my brain, and am often in the best sense active when I present the appearance of a heedless and out-of-work, negligent, dreamy, and idle pickpocket, lost out in the blue, or in the green, making the worst impression, seeming a frivolous man devoid of any sense of responsibility? Mysterious and secretly there prowl at the walker's heels all kinds of beautiful subtle walker's thoughts, such as make him stand in his ardent and regardless tracks and listen, so that he will again and again be confused and startled by curious impressions and bewitchings of spirit power, and he has the feeling that he must sink all of a sudden into the earth, or that before his dazzled, bewildered thinker's and poet's eyes an abyss has opened. His head wants to fall off, and his otherwise so lively arms and legs are as benumbed. Countryside and people, sounds and colors, faces and farms, clouds and sunlight swirl all around him like diagrams, and he must ask himself: "Where am I?" Earth and heaven suddenly stream together and collide, rocking interlocked one upon the other into a flashing, shimmering, obscure nebular imagery; chaos begins, and the orders vanish. Convulsed, he laboriously tries to retain his normal state of mind; he succeeds, and he walks on, full of confidence. Do you think it quite impossible that on a gentle and patient walk I should meet giants, have the privilege of seeing professors, do business in passing with booksellers and bank officials, converse with budding, youthful songstresses and former actresses, dine at noon with intelligent ladies, stroll through woods, dispatch dangerous letters, and come to wild blows with spiteful, ironic master tailors? All this can happen, and I believe it actually did happen. There accompanies the walker always something remarkable, some food for thought,

something fantastic, and he would be foolish if he did not notice this spiritual side, or even thrust it away; rather, he wel-
comes all curious and peculiar phenomena, becomes their
friend and brother, because they delight him; he makes them
into formed and substantial bodies, gives them structure and
soul just as they for their part instruct and inspire him. In a
word, by thinking, pondering, drilling, digging, speculating,
writing, investigating, researching, and walking, I earn my
daily bread with as much sweat on my brow as anybody. Although I may cut a most carefree figure, I am highly serious
and conscientious, and though I seem to be no more than delicate and dreamy, I am a solid technician! I hope that all these
meticulous explanations convince you that my endeavors are
honorable, and satisfy you completely."

The official said: "Good!" and he added: "Your application
concerning approval of an exceptionally low rate of taxation
we shall examine later and inform you shortly of the reduction
or approval thereof as may be. For the kind declaration delivered and the industriously assembled honest statements we
thank you. For the present you may withdraw and ·proceed
with your walk."

As I was mercifully released, I hurried happily away, and
was soon in the open air again. Raptures of freedom seized me
and carried me away. I come now at last, after many a bravely
endured adventure, and after more or less victoriously overwhelming many an arduous obstacle, to the long-since announced and forecast railway crossing, where I had to stop a
while to wait pleasantly until gradually the train kindly had
the high grace to pass gently by. All sorts of male and
female folk of every age and character were standing and waiting at the barrier, as did I. The kindly, corpulent signalman's
wife stood there still as a statue and examined us loiterers and
waiters thoroughly. Hurtling past, the railway train was full of
soldiery, and all the soldiers, sworn and dedicated to serve
their dearly beloved fatherland, looking out at the windows,
this entire traveling military college on the one hand and the
useless civilian population on the other greeted each other and

waved their hands amicably and patriotically, an action which spread pleasant feelings far and wide. As the crossing was now open, I and all the others went peacefully on our ways, and now all the world around seemed to me suddenly to have become a thousand times more beautiful. The walk seemed to be becoming more beautiful, rich, and long. Here at the railway crossing seemed to be the peak, or something like the center, from which again the gentle declivity would begin. Something akin to sorrow's golden bliss and melancholy's magic breathed around me like a quiet, lofty god. "It is divinely beautiful here," I said to myself. Like a song at departure that brings tears to our eyes, the gentle countryside lay there with its dear humble fields, gardens, and houses. Soft, very ancient folk lamentations and the sorrows of the good, poor folk thronged and sounded everywhere. Spirits with enchanting shapes and garments emerged vast and soft, and the dear good country road shone sky-blue, and white, and precious gold. Compassion and enchantment flew like carven angels falling from heaven over the gold-colored, rosey-aureoled little houses of the poor, which the sunlight delicately embraced and framed about. Love and poverty and silvery-golden breath walked and floated hand in hand. I felt as if someone I loved were calling me by name, or as if someone were kissing and comforting me. God the Almighty, our merciful Lord, walked down the road, to glorify it and make it divinely beautiful. Imaginings of all sorts, and illusions, made me believe that Jesus Christ was risen again and wandering now in the midst of the people and in the midst of this friendly place. Houses, gardens, and people were transfigured into musical sounds, all that was solid seemed to be transfigured into soul and into gentleness. Sweet veils of silver and soul-haze swam through all things and lay over all things. The soul of the world had opened, and all grief, all human disappointment, all evil, all pain seemed to vanish, from now on never to appear again. Earlier walks came before my eyes; but the wonderful image of the humble present became a feeling which overpowered all others. The future paled, and the past dissolved. I glowed and flowered myself in the glow-

ing, flowering present. From near and far, great things and
small things emerged bright silver with marvelous gestures,
joys, and enrichments, and in the midst of this beautiful place I
dreamed of nothing but this place itself. All other fantasies
sank and vanished in meaninglessness. I had the whole rich
earth immediately before me, and I still looked only at what
was most small and most humble. With gestures of love the
heavens rose and fell. I had become an inward being, and I
walked as in an inward world; everything outside me became a
dream; what I had understood till now became unintelligible. I
fell away from the surface, down into the fabulous depths,
which I recognized then to be all that was good. What we
understand and love understands and loves us also. I was no
longer myself, was another, and yet it was on this account that
I became properly myself. In the sweet light of love I realized,
or believed I realized, that perhaps the inward self is the only
self which really exists. The thought seized me: "Where would
we poor people be, if there was no earth faithful to us? What
would we have, if we did not have this beauty and this good?
Where would I be, if I was not here? Here I have everything,
and elsewhere I would have nothing."

What I saw was as small and poor as it was large and significant, as modest as it was charming, as near as it was good, and
as delightful as it was warm. Two houses which lay close together in the bright sunlight, like lively and kindly neighbors,
these I delighted in. One delight followed the other, and in the
soft confiding air contentment floated to and fro and trembled
as with joy restrained. One of the two subtle little houses was
the Bear Inn; the bear was admirably and comically depicted
on the inn sign. Chestnut trees overshadowed the delicate and
pretty house, which was assuredly inhabited by kind, pleasant,
friendly people; it did not seem, like some buildings, to be
arrogant, but rather the very image of intimacy and trust.
Everywhere the eye looked lay splendid profusion of contented
gardens, hovered green tangled profusion of pleasant leaves.
The second house, or cottage, in its evident delightfulness and
humility, was like a childishly beautiful page out of a picture

book, a sweet illustration, so charming and curious did it show itself to be. The vicinity of the cottage seemed entirely beautiful and good. I fell immediately head over heels in love with this pretty little house person, and I would have passionately liked to go into it, in order to make my nest and lodging there and to live in the magic cottage, the jewel, forever and content; but it is unfortunately just the most beautiful houses which are occupied, and the person who looks for a dwelling to suit his presumptuous tastes has a difficult time, because that which is empty and available is often frightful and inspires horror. The pretty cottage was certainly inhabited by a little spinster or grandmother; it had about it just such a smell, just such a look. It being permitted to say so, I report in addition that on the wall of the cottage abounded wall paintings, or noble frescoes, which were divinely subtle and amusing and showed a Swiss alpine landscape in which stood, painted again, another house, to be accurate a Bernese mountain farmhouse. Frankly, the painting was not good at all. It would be impudent to maintain that it was. But, nonetheless, to me it seemed marvelous. Plain and simple as it was, it enchanted me; as a matter of fact, any sort of painting enchants me, however foolish and clumsy it is, because every painting reminds me first of diligence and industry, and second of Holland. Is not all music, even the most niggardly, beautiful to the person who loves the very being and existence of music? Is not almost any human being you please, even the worst and most unpleasant, lovable to the person who is a friend to man? Painted landscape in the middle of real landscape is capricious, piquant. This nobody will contest. The fact that a little old lady may live in the cottage I certainly did not anyway confirm or establish on record, and I have no desire at all to give it as gospel. But I am surprised at myself that I should dare to use the word "fact" here, where everything is, or should be, supple and as full of human nature as the thoughts and feelings of a mother's heart. Further, the cottage was painted blue-gray and had bright golden-green shutters, which seemed to smile, and all around it in the magic garden was a fragrance of most beautiful flowers. Over the little garden- or summerhouse there bowed and twisted with enchanting grace a rosebush or bouquet full of the loveliest roses.

Assuming I am not delirious, but hale and hearty, as I hope and would not like to doubt I am, proceeding gently on my way I passed by a country barbershop, with whose contents and owner, however, I have, it seems to me, no cause to concern myself, because I am of the opinion that it is not yet urgently necessary for me to have my hair cut, though this would be perhaps quite jolly and amusing. Further, I passed by a cobbler's workshop, which reminded me of the poet Lenz, a genius, but unhappy, who learned to make, and made, shoes while his soul and spirit were unhinged. Did I not also look in passing into a schoolhouse and into a friendly schoolroom, exactly when the schoolmistress was issuing questions and commands? This is a favorable occasion on which to remark how eagerly the walker for an instant wished he might once more be a child and a disobedient, mischievous schoolboy, go to school again and be able to harvest and receive a well-earned thrashing in punishment for naughtinesses and outrages committed. Speaking of thrashings, our opinion might here be mentioned and interlarded that a countryman deserves to be well and truly thrashed, if he is not hesitant to cut down the pride of the landscape and the glory of his own hearth and home, namely his high and ancient nut tree, in order to trade it in for despicable, wicked, foolish money. For I passed by a very lovely farmhouse, with a high, splendid, and luxuriant nut tree; and here the thought of trading and thrashing rose in my mind. "This high majestical tree," I cried aloud, "which protects and beautifies this house so wonderfully, spinning for it a cage of such serious, joyous homeliness and intimate domesticity, this tree, I say, is a divinity, a holy thing, and a thousand lashes to the unfeeling and impious owner of it if he dare make all this golden, divinely green magic of leaves vanish to gratify his thirst for money, which is the vilest and most contemptible thing on earth. Such cretins should be kicked out of the parish. To Siberia or Tierra del Fuego with such defilers and destroyers of what is beautiful. But, thank God, there are also farmers who have hearts and senses for what is delicate and good."

As regards the tree, the greed, the countryman, the transpor-
tation to Siberia, and the thrashing which the countryman
apparently deserves because he fells the tree, I have perhaps
gone too far, and I must confess that I let my indignation
carry me away. Friends of beautiful trees will nevertheless
understand my displeasure, and agree with my so energetically
expressed regret. For all I care, the thousand lashes can be
returned to me forthwith. To the expression "cretin" I myself
deny applause. The expression is coarse, and I dislike it, and I
therefore beg the reader's forgiveness. As I have already had
to beg his forgiveness several times, I have become quite a dab
hand at self-excuse. "Unfeeling and impious owner" also I had
no real need to say. The mind gets overheated, and this ought
to be avoided. That is obvious. My grief over the downfall of a
beautiful, tall, ancient tree can still stand, and I certainly make
the worst of it; nobody can hinder me from that. "Kicked out of
the parish" is an improvident phrase, and as for the thirst for
money, which I have called vile, I suppose that I have myself
at some time or another offended, fallen short, and sinned in
this respect, and that certain wretchednesses and vilenesses
have not remained utterly alien and unknown to me. These
words show that I practice a policy of softheartedness, which
has a beauty that is not to be found anywhere else; but I consider this policy to be indispensable. Propriety enjoins us to be
careful to deal as severely with ourselves as with others, and to
judge others as mildly and gently as we judge ourselves, which
latter we do, as is well known, at all times instinctively. It is
delicious, is it not, the way I neatly correct my mistakes and
smooth over the offenses? In making admissions I prove myself
peace-loving, and in rounding off the angles and making soft
what is rough I am a subtle, delicate attenuator, show a sense
of good tone, and am diplomatic. Of course I have disgraced
myself; but I hope that my good will is appreciated.

If anybody still says now that I am indiscreet, imperious,
and a despot blundering about at will, then I maintain, that is
to say, I dare to hope that I have the right to maintain, that the

person who says such a thing is sorely mistaken. With such continual considerateness and gentility, perhaps no other author has ever thought of the reader.

Well, now I can obligingly attend to a château and aristocratic palace, and as follows: I politely play my trump card; for with a half-ruined stately home and patrician house, with an age-gray, park-surrounded, proud knight's castle and lordly residence such as now enters my view, one can make a great song and dance, excite respect, arouse envy, inspire wonder, and pocket the proceeds. Many a poor but elegant man of letters would live with the greatest of pleasure, the highest satisfaction, in such a castle, or stronghold, with courtyard and drive for haughty carriages embossed with coats-of-arms. Many a poor but pleasure-loving painter dreams of residing temporarily on delicious old-fashioned country estates. Many a city girl, educated but perhaps poor as a church mouse, thinks with melancholy rapture and idealistic fervor of ponds, grottoes, high chambers and placidities, and of herself waited upon by hurrying footmen and noble-minded knights. On the lordly residence I saw here, that is, rather in it than on it, could be read the date 1709, which naturally quickened and intensified my interest. With a certain rapture I looked as a naturalist and antiquary into the dreaming, ancient, curious garden, where, in a pool with a pleasant splashing fountain, I discovered and proved with ease the presence of a most peculiar fish, which was one meter in length; namely, a solitary sheatfish. Likewise I saw and established with romantic bliss the presence of a garden pavilion in Moorish or Arabian style, beautifully and opulently painted in sky-blue, mysterious star-silver, gold, brown, and noble, serious black. I supposed and sensed at once with the most subtle intelligence that the pavilion must date from, and have been erected in, about the year 1858, a deduction, conjecture, and scenting-out which perhaps entitles me sometimes confidently to read with a rather complacent expression on my face, and in a rather self-confident manner, a pertinent paper on the subject in the Town Hall Chambers, before a large and enthusiastic public. Then very probably the press would mention my paper, which could only mean an extreme pleasure for me; since sometimes it mentions all sorts of things with not even one small dying word. As I was studying the Arabian or Persian garden pavilion, it occurred to me to think: "How beautiful it must be here at night, when everything is veiled in an almost impenetrable darkness, when all around it is quiet, black, and soundless, pines gently towering out of the darkness, midnight feelings arrest the solitary wanderer, and now a lamp, which spreads a sweet yellow light, is brought into the pavilion by a beautiful, richly jeweled noblewoman, who then, impelled by her peculiar whim and moved by a curious access of soul, begins, at the piano, with which in this case our summerhouse must naturally be equipped, to play music to which, if the dream be permitted, she sings in a delightfully beautiful, pure voice. How one would listen there, how one would dream, how happy one would be made by this night music!"

But it was not midnight and far and wide neither a courtly Middle Ages nor a year 1500 or 1700, but broad daylight and a working day, and a troupe of people, together with a most uncourtly and unknightly, most crude and most impertinent automobile, which came my way, rudely disturbed me at my wealth of learned and romantic observations, and threw me in a trice out of the domain of castle poetry and reverie on things past, so that I cried out instinctively: "It really is most vulgar the way people impede me here from making my elegant studies and from plunging into the most superb profundities. I could be indignant; but instead I would rather be meek, and suffer, and endure with a good grace. Sweet is thought about beauty and loveliness that are passed away, sweet is the noble, pale image of drowned and perished beauty; but on the world around and on one's fellow men one has not therefore the right to turn one's back, and one may not think that one is entitled to resent people and their contrivances because they disregard the state of mind of him who is absorbed in the realms of history and thought."

"A thunderstorm," I thought as I walked on, "would be beautiful here. I hope I shall have the opportunity to experience one."

To a good honest jet-black dog who lay in the road I delivered the following facetious address: "Does it not enter your mind, you apparently quite unschooled and uncultivated fellow, to stand up and offer me your coal-black paw, though you must see from my gait and entire conduct that I am a person who has lived a full seven years at least in the capital of this country and of the world, and who during this time has not one minute, let alone one hour, or one month, or one week, been out of touch or out of pleasant intercourse with exclusively cultured people? Where, ragamuffin, were you brought up? And you do not answer me a word? You lie where you are, look at me calmly, move not a finger, and remain as motionless as a monument? You should be ashamed of yourself!"

Yet actually I liked the dog, who in the loyal-hearted watchfulness and humorous repose and composure he displayed looked magnificent, uncommonly good, and because his eyes twinkled at me so merrily, I spoke with him, and because he really did not understand a word, I could venture to scold him, which however, as will have been observed from the comic manner of my address, cannot anyway have been meant unkindly.

Catching sight of an elegant, well-starched gentleman strutting and waddling and prancing toward me, I had the melancholy thought: "And poor little ill-dressed neglected children? Is it possible that such a well-dressed, elaborately groomed, splendidly tailored and upholstered, beringed and jewel-behung, spick-and-span beau of a gentleman does not give a moment's thought to poor young creatures who go about often enough in rags, show a sad lack of care and attention, and are lamentably neglected? Is the peacock not a little uneasy? Does this Adult Gentleman who goes about so beautifully not feel in any way whatsoever concerned when he sees dirty speckled little children? It seems to me that no mature man ought to want to appear all elegance as long as there are children who have no finery to wear at all."

But one might have just as much right to say that nobody ought to go to concerts, or visit the theater, or enjoy any other kind of amusement as long as there are prisons in the world and places of punishment with unhappy prisoners in them. This is of course asking too much. And if anyone were to wait content and enjoying life until finally the world should contain no more poor miserable people, then he would be waiting until the gray impenetrable end of all time, and until the ice-cold empty end of the world, and by then all joy and life itself would in all probability be utterly gone from him.

A disheveled, discomfited, spent, and tremulous charwoman, extraordinarily weak and weary, and yet hurrying along because she evidently still had many more things to do, reminded me for an instant of spoiled, pampered little girls, or larger girls, who are often ignorant, or seem to know what sort of delicate elegant occupation or diversion to pass the day with, and who perhaps are never thoroughly tired, who consider all day and for weeks on end what they can wear to increase the polish of their appearance, and who have time and to spare for long meditations on the subject, whence continually more and more exaggerated refinements wrap round their persons and sweet confectionlike little forms.

But I am myself usually a lover and admirer of such amiable, utterly pampered moonbeam maidens, beautiful, delicate, plantlike girls. A charming young thing could command of me whatever might occur to her, I would blindly obey her. Oh, how beautiful beauty is, and how charming is charm!

Once more I return to the topic of architecture and building, and here a bit, or spot, of art and literature will need consideration.

But first a note: the cleaning of ancient, noble, dignified, historic places and buildings, with their traceries of ornamental flowers, reveals considerable bad taste. Whoever does this, or causes it to be done, sins against the spirit of dignity and beauty, and injures the lovely remembrance of ancestors, who were as brave as they were noble. Second, never garland and conceal the architecture of fountains with flowers. Of course, flowers in themselves are beautiful; but they do not exist to declarify and erase the noble austerity and austere beauty of images in stone. At any time the predilection for flowers can deteriorate into a foolish mania. Personalities, magistrates, whom this concerns, may make inquiries in the authoritative circles as to whether I am right, and thereafter be kind enough to behave nicely.

To mention two beautiful and interesting edfices, which powerfully arrested me and claimed my attention to an unusual degree, it may be said that as I followed my road farther I came to a delightful, curious chapel, which I immediately named Brentano's Chapel, because I saw that it dated from the fantastical, golden-aureoled, half-bright and half-dark age of the Romantics. I recalled Brentano's great wild, dark, temptestuous novel *Godwi*. Lofty, slender, arched windows gave this most original and peculiar building a delicate, delightful appearance, and laid upon it the spirit of enchantment, spirit of inwardness and the meditative life. There came to my mind fiery and profound landscape descriptions by the poet mentioned above, particularly the account of German oak forests. Soon after this I was standing in front of a villa called Terrasse, which reminded me of the painter Karl Stauffer-Bern, who lived and stayed here for a time, and, simultaneously, of certain very superb, noble edifices which lie on the Tiergartenstrasse in Berlin, and which, owing to the austere, majestical, and simple classical style to which they give expression, are congenial and worth seeing. To me, Stauffer's House and Brentano's Chapel were monuments to two worlds which are to be strictly distinguished from each other, each being in its curious way graceful, entertaining, and significant: here a measured, cool elegance; there the exuberant, deep-minded dream, here something subtle and beautiful, and there something subtle and beautiful, but in substance and structure completely different from the other, although each lies near to the other in point of time. Evening is now gradually beginning to fall upon my walk, and its quiet end, I think, cannot any more be very far away.

Perhaps this is just the place for a few everyday things and street events, each in its turn: a splendid piano factory and also other factories and company buildings; an avenue of poplars close beside a black river, men, women, children, electric trams croaking along, each with a responsible field marshal or general peering out, a troupe of charmingly chequered and spotted pale-colored cows, peasant women on farm carts, and the rolling of wheels and cracking of whips thereto appertaining, several heavily laden, high-towering beer wagons and beer barrels, homeward-bound workers streaming and storming out of the factories, the overwhelming sight and actuality of all this mass, and the relevant curious thoughts; goods wagons with goods, coming from the goods station, an entire traveling and wandering circus with elephants, horses, dogs, zebras, giraffes, fierce lions locked in lion cages, with Singalese, Indians, tigers, monkeys, and creepy-crawly crocodiles, girl rope dancers and polar bears, and all the requisite opulence of camp followers, servants, packs of performers and staff; further: boys armed with wooden rifles, imitating the European War as they unleash all the furies of war, a small scoundrel singing the song "One Hundred Thousand Frogs," of which he is mightily proud; further: foresters and woodsmen with trucks full of wood, two or three splendid pigs, whereat the lively imagination of the observer greedily paints him a picture of the deliciousness and acceptability of a marvelously redolent, already roast joint of pork, which is understandable; a farmhouse with a motto over the entrance, two Bohemian, Galician, Slav, Wend, or even gypsy girls in red boots and with jet-black eyes and ditto hair, at the sight of whom one thinks perhaps of the plummy novel *The Gypsy Princess*, which actually happens in Hungary, though it makes little difference, or of *Preziosa*, which is of course of Spanish origin, but there is no need to take it literally. Further, in the way of shops: paper, meat, clock, shoe, hat, iron, cloth, grocery, spice, fancy goods, millinery, bakery, and confectionery shops. And everywhere on all these things delicious evening sun. Further, much noise and uproar, schools and schoolteachers, the latter with weighty and

dignified faces, landscapes and air and much else that is picturesque. Further, not to be overlooked or forgotten: signs and
advertisements, as: "Persil," or "Maggi's Unsurpassed Soups,"
or "Continental Rubber Heels Enormously Durable," or "Free-
hold Property for Sale," or "The Best Milk Chocolate," and I
honestly know not what else. If one were to count until everything had been accurately enumerated, one would never reach
the end. People with insight feel and observe this fact. A
placard or board struck me especially; it read as follows:

"FULL BOARD AND LODGING

or elegant gentlemen's *pension* recommends to elegant or at
least better-off gentlemen its first-class cuisine, which is such
that we can with a clear conscience say that it will gratify the
most pampered palate and delight the liveliest appetite. Nevertheless, preferably we decline to consider all-too-hungry
stomachs. The culinary art we offer is adjusted to higher
education, by which we hope to indicate that we are pleased to
see only really well-educated gentlemen banqueting at our
tables. Rascals who drink their weekly or monthly wage, and
who are thus unable to pay promptly, we have not the remotest
desire to meet; rather, in respect of our honored guests, we
insist on delicate conduct and pleasing manners. Charming,
polite young ladies are in our house in attendance at the deliciously laid, tasteful tables, which are decorated with all sorts
of flowers. We make this clear, so that Prospective Gentlemen
may understand that elegant behavior and really jolly and correct conduct are required of the likely resident from the moment he sets foot in our estimable, respectable establishment.
With libertines and rowdies, boasters and swaggerers we quite
resolutely refuse all contact. Such persons who have cause to
believe that they are of this type will be so good as to remain at
a distance from our first-rate institute and spare us their objectionable presences. Every nice, delicate, polite, courteous, elegant, obliging, friendly, cheerful, not excessively gay and
cheerful but rather quiet, above all solvent, steady, punctually
paying gentleman guest, on the other hand, will really be in

every respect welcome, and he will be attended to most elegantly and treated as courteously and nicely as is humanly possible; this we promise faithfully, and we intend to keep this promise continually, the pleasure is ours. Such a nice, charming gentleman will find at our tables delicacies whose like he would have great trouble to find elsewhere; for from our exquisite cuisine proceed veritable masterpieces of culinary art; this everyone will have the occasion to prove who wishes to sample our excellent Gentlemen's Pension to which we heartily extend our invitation at all times. The food which we place on our tables surpasses in quality as in quantity all reasonably healthy belief, and no fantasy, however strong, can even approximately conceive the delectable, luscious tidbits which we are accustomed to bring forth and display before the joyfully astonished eyes of gentlemen diners here assembled. But, as has already been stressed several times, only gentlemen of the better type come into consideration, and we take the liberty, in order to avoid errors and to remove doubts, of publishing our conception of such persons: in our eyes, he alone is a gentleman of the better type who seethes with elegance and superiority, and who is just simply far better than the other ordinary people. People who are no more than ordinary do not suit us at all. A gentleman of the better type is, in our opinion, only he who entertains a fair number of vain and foolish ideas about himself, and who above all imagines that his nose is better than any other good and sensible human nose whatsoever. The conduct of a gentleman of the better type clearly exhibits this peculiar prerequisite, and it is upon this that we rely. Whoever is merely good, upright, and honorable, and shows no other important merits, should not trouble us; for to us he does not seem to be a gentleman of the more elegant, of the better type. For the selection of only the most elegant and superior gentlemen of the better type, we possess the most subtle intelligence. We can see at once from the gait, the tone of voice, from the way of making conversation, from the features of the face, from the movements of the body, and particularly from the clothes, the hat, the stick, the flower in the buttonhole, which either exists or does not, whether a gentleman belongs among the better gentlemen, or does not. The acumen we possess in this respect borders on magic, and we make so bold as to contend that we credit ourselves with a certain genius in these matters. Well, now it is clear what sort of gentlemen we indicate, and if a person comes to us and we can tell from afar that he is unsuitable for us and our establishment, then we tell him: 'We very much regret, and we are really very sorry.' "

Two or three readers will perhaps raise a few doubts about the authenticity of this notice, insofar as they will tell themselves that it is hardly believable.

Perhaps there were a few repetitions here and there. But I would like to confess that I consider man and nature to be in lovely and charming flight from repetitions, and I would like further to confess that I regard this phenomenon as a beauty and a blessing. Of course, one finds in some places sensation-hungry novelty hunters and novelty worshippers, spoiled by overexcitement, people who almost every instant covet joys that have never been seen before. The writer does not write for such people, nor does the composer compose for them, nor does the painter paint for them. On the whole I consider the constant need for delight and diversion in completely new things to be a sign of pettiness, lack of inner life, of estrangement from nature, and of a mediocre or defective gift of understanding. It is little children for whom one must always be producing something new and different, only in order to stop their being dissatisfied. The serious writer does not feel called upon to supply accumulations of material, to act the agile servant of nervous greed; and consequently he is not afraid of a few natural repetitions, although of course he takes continual trouble to forfend too many similarities.

It was now evening and I came to a quiet, pretty path or side road which ran under trees, toward the lake, and here the walk ended. In a forest of alders, at the water's edge, a school for boys and girls had assembled and the parson or teacher was giving instruction in botany and the observation of nature, here in the midst of nature, at nightfall. As I walked slowly onward, two human figures arose in my mind. Perhaps because of a certain general weariness, I thought of a beautiful girl, and of how alone I was in the wide world, and that this could not be quite right. Self-reproof touched me from behind my back and stood before me in my way, and I had to struggle hard. Certain evil memories took control of me. Self-accusations made my heart deeply and suddenly a burden to me. Flowers meanwhile I searched for and picked all around me, partly in the little forest, partly in the fields. Gently and softly it began to rain, whereupon the delicate countryside became even more delicate and still. It seemed to me that tears fell, and while I was gathering flowers I listened to the soft weeping which rustled down upon the leaves. Warm, gentle summer rain, how sweet you are! "Why am I picking flowers here?" I asked myself, and looked down pensively to the ground, and the delicate rain increased my pensiveness till it became sorrow. Old, long-past failures occurred to me, disloyalty, hatred, scorn, falsity, cunning, anger, and many violent unbeautiful actions. Uncontrolled passion, wild desire, and how I had hurt people sometimes, and done wrong. Like a packed stage of scenes from a drama my past life opened to me, and I was seized with astonishment at my countless frailties, at all unfriendliness and lovelessness which I had caused people to feel. Then there came before my eyes the second figure, and suddenly I saw again the poor, weary old forsaken man whom I had seen a few days before, lying on the ground in the forest, and he looked up, so pitiful, deathly and pale, lamentable, so sorrowful and weary to death, that the sad sight of him had terrified me and choked my soul. This weary man I now saw in my mind's eye, and a feeling of weakness took hold of me. I felt the need to lie down somewhere, and since a friendly, cozy little place by the lakeside was nearby, I made myself comfortable, somewhat tired as I was, on the soft ground under the artless branches of a tree. As I looked at earth and air and sky the melancholy unquestioning thought came to me that I was a poor prisoner between heaven and earth, that all men were miserably im-

prisoned in this way, that for all men there was only the one
dark path into the other world, the path down into the pit, into
the earth, that there was no other way into the other world
than that which led through the grave. "So then everything,
everything, all this rich life, the friendly, thoughtful colors,
this delight, this joy and pleasure in life, all these human mean-
ings, family, friend, and beloved, this bright, tender air full of
divinely beautiful images, houses of fathers, houses of mothers,
and dear gentle roads, must one day pass away and die, the
high sun, the moon, and the hearts and eyes of men." For a
long time I thought of this, and asked those people whom perhaps I might have injured to forgive me. For a long time I lay
there in unclear thought, until I remembered the girl again,
who was so beautiful and fresh with youth, and had such soft,
good, pure eyes. I vividly imagined how charming was her
childish, pretty mouth, how pretty her cheeks, and how with
its melodious sweetness her bodily form had enchanted me,
how I had asked her a question a while ago, how in her doubt
and disbelief her lovely eyes had looked away, and how she
had said no when I asked her if she believed in my sincere
love, affection, surrender, and tenderness. The situation had
obliged her to travel, and she had gone away. Perhaps I would
still have had time to convince her that I meant well with her,
that her dear person was important to me, and that I had many
beautiful reasons for wanting to make her happy, and thus
myself happy also; but I had thought no more of it, and she
went away. Why then the flowers? "Did I pick flowers to lay
them upon my sorrow?" I asked myself, and the flowers fell out
of my hand. I had risen up, to go home; for it was late now, and
everything was dark.

[1917]

So! I've Got You

ONE who could not trust his eyes looked at the door of a room to see if it was closed. Indeed it was closed, and properly to be sure, there was no reason to doubt it. The door was definitely closed, but he who did not trust his eyes did not believe it, sniffed about the door with his nose, so that he could smell if it was closed or not. It was really and truly closed. Without question it was closed. It was by no means open. By all means it was closed. Undoubtedly the door was closed. Doubt was in no way to be feared; he who did not trust his eyes, however, doubted strongly that the door was actually closed, although he clearly saw how tightly it was shut. It was as tightly shut as those doors which cannot on the whole be shut any tighter, but he who did not trust his eyes was still a long way from being convinced of that. He stared hard at the door and asked it if it was closed. "Door, tell me, are you closed?" he asked, but the door gave no answer. It was, anyway, not at all necessary that it answered, since it was closed. The door was perfectly in order, but he who did not trust his eyes did not trust the door, did not believe that it was in order, continued to doubt that it was in order. "Are you really shut or are you not shut?" he asked again, but of course the door anew gave no answer. Can one demand of a door that it give an

answer? Again the door was looked at suspiciously to find out
if it was truly closed. At last he comprehended that it was
closed, at last he was convinced of it. Thereupon he laughed
loudly, was very happy that he could laugh, and said to the
door: "So! I've got you," and with this fine expression he was
satisfied and went to his daily work. Is not such a person a
fool? Certainly! but he was just one who doubted everything.

Once he wrote a letter. After he had it quite ready, i.e., had
completely finished it, he looked askance at the letter, for once
again he did not trust his eyes and was not close to believing he
had written a letter. The letter had, however, certainly been
written, there was no doubt about it, but, as with the door, he
who did not trust his eyes sniffed about the letter with his nose,
was the height of suspicion and wondered if the letter was
really written now or not. Without doubt it was written, it was
definitely written, but he who did not trust his eyes was in
no way convinced of it, rather he smelled, as I said, cautiously
and carefully around the letter and asked in a loud cry: "Letter, tell me, are you written or not?" The letter naturally did
not give the slightest answer. Since when can letters give
speeches and answers? The letter was perfectly in order, quite
ready, readable, and nicely written word by word, sentence by
sentence. Splendid and proper stood the letters, periods, com-
mas, semicolons, question marks, and exclamation points, and
the delicate quotation marks all in place. Not a dot on an *i*
was missing in the great work; he, however, who had written
the masterpiece of a letter and unfortunately did not trust his
eyes, was in no way convinced of all that, rather asked anew:
"Are you in order, letter?" It gave, however, no answer again,
naturally. For that it was again looked askance at and considered obliquely. At last the dumb person knew he had really
and truly written the letter, and for that reason laughed joyfully and loudly, was happy like a small child, rubbed his
hands full of pleasure, folded the letter together, stuck it
exultantly in a suitable envelope, and said: "So! I've got you,"
about which fine expression he was uncommonly delighted.
Thereupon he went to his daily work. Is not such a person a

fool? Indeed, but he was just one who believed in nothing, one who did not come out from sorrows, distress, and doubt, one who, as I said, doubted everything.

One other time, he wanted to drink a glass of red wine which was before him, but he wouldn't dare do it, because again he did not trust his eyes. No doubt there was the glass of wine. Without doubt, the glass of wine stood there in every respect, and the question, if it stood there or did not stand there, was thoroughly absurd and silly. Any average person would have immediately comprehended the glass of wine, but he who did not trust his eyes did not comprehend it, did not believe it, looked at the glass of wine for a good half hour, sniffed about it with his fool nose a meter long, as with the letter, and asked: "Glass of wine, tell me, are you really there or are you really not there?" The question was superfluous, since the glass of wine was there, that was fact. It gave no answer, naturally, to the dumb question. A glass of wine gives no answer, it is simply there and wants to be drunk, which is better than all talking and answering. Our good glass of wine was suspiciously sniffed at with the nose from all sides, like the letter before, and stared at with the eyes, like the door before. "Are you at bottom there, or aren't you there?" was asked again, and again no answer was forthcoming. "So drink it then, so taste it, let yourself enjoy it, then you will have felt and experienced it, and its existence will no longer be in doubt to you," one would have liked to shout at him, him who did not trust his eyes, who looked at the glass of wine mistrustfully, instead of putting it to his lips. He was still a long way from being convinced. He went into still more delicate and lengthy details; at last, however, he seemed to have comprehended it, finally he believed that there was in fact a glass of wine under his nose. "So! I've got you," he said, laughed loudly like a child, rubbed his hands again in pleasure, smacked his tongue, gave himself a sound slap on the head out of purely foolish and immense joy, took the glass of wine carefully into his hands and drank it up, was satisfied at that, and thereupon went to his daily work. Is not such a person an arrant fool? Surely, but he was just one who did not trust his ears or eyes, one who did not have a single calm minute due to sincerely sensitive and overly sensitive deliberation, one who was unhappy whenever the least thing failed to pass or work exactly, a fool for order and punctuality, a fool for accuracy and precision, one who should have been sent and driven into a School of Thoughtlessness, one who, in God's name, as I said, doubted everything.

[1917]

Translated by Tom Whalen and Carol Gehrig

Nothing at All

A WOMAN who was only just a little flighty went to town to buy something good for supper for herself and her husband. Of course, many a woman has gone shopping and in so doing been just a little absentminded. So in no way is this story new; all the same, I shall continue and relate that the woman who had wanted to buy something good for supper for herself and her husband and for this reason had gone to town did not exactly have her mind on the matter. Over and over she considered what delights and delicacies she could buy for herself and her husband, but since she didn't, as already mentioned, exactly have her mind on the matter and was a little absentminded, she came to no decision, and it seemed that she did not exactly know what she really wanted. "It must be something that can be made quickly since it's already late, my time is limited," she thought. God! She was, you know, only just a little flighty and did not exactly have her mind on the matter. Impartiality and objectivity are fine and good. But the woman here was not particularly objective, rather a little absentminded and flighty. Over and over she considered but came, as already mentioned, to no decision. The ability to make a decision is fine and good. But this woman possessed no such ability. She wanted to buy something really good and delicious for herself and her husband to eat. And for this fine reason she went to town; but she simply did not succeed, she simply did not succeed. Over and over she considered. She wasn't lacking in good will, she certainly wasn't lacking in good intentions, she was just a little flighty, didn't have her mind on the matter, and therefore didn't succeed. It isn't good when minds aren't on the matter, and, in a word, the woman finally got disgusted, and she went home with nothing at all.

"What delicious and good, exquisite and fine, sensible and intelligent food did you buy for supper?" asked the husband when he saw his good-looking, nice little wife come home.

She replied: "I bought nothing at all."

"How's that?" asked the husband.

She said: "Over and over I considered, but came to no decision, because the choice was too difficult for me to make. Also it was already late, and my time was limited. I wasn't lacking in good will or the best of all intentions, but I just didn't have my mind on the matter. Believe me, dear husband, it's really terrible when you don't keep your mind on a matter. It seems that I was only just a little flighty and because of that I didn't succeed. I went to town and I wanted to buy something truly delicious and good for me and you, I wasn't lacking in good will, over and over I considered, but the choice was too difficult and my mind wasn't on the matter, and therefore I didn't succeed, and therefore I bought nothing at all. We will have to be satisfied today with nothing at all for once, won't we. Nothing at all can be prepared most quickly and, at any rate, doesn't cause indigestion. Should you be angry with me for this? I can't believe that."

So for once, or for a change, they ate nothing at all at night, and the good upright husband was in no way angry, he was too chivalrous, too mannerly, and too well-behaved for that. He would never have dared to make an unpleasant face, he was much too cultivated. A good husband doesn't do something like that. And so they ate nothing at all and were both satisfied, for it tasted exceptionally good to them. His wife's idea to prefer nothing at all for a change the good husband found quite charming, and while he maintained that he was convinced she had had a delightful inspiration, he feigned his great joy, whereby he indeed concealed how welcome a nutritious, honest supper like, e.g., a hearty, valiant apple mash would have been.

Many other things would have probably tasted better to him than nothing at all.

[1917]

Translated by Tom Whalen and Carol Gehrig

Kienast

KIENAST was the name of a man who wanted nothing to do with anything. Even in his youth he stood out unpleasantly as an unwilling sort. As a child he gave his parents much grief, and later, as a citizen, his fellow citizens. It didn't matter what time of day you wanted to talk to him, you would never get from him a friendly or fellowly word. Indignant, invidious was his behavior, and his conduct was repulsive. Guys like this Kienast probably believed it a sacrilege if they were kind or obliging to people. But have no fear: he was neither kind nor courteous. Of that he wanted to hear nothing. "Nonsense," he grumbled at everything desiring his attention. "I'm really sorry, but I have no time," he was in the habit of angrily mumbling as soon as someone came to him with a request. Those were duped folks who went to Kienast with a request. They didn't get much from him, because there was no trace of considerateness to be found in him. He didn't want to know even the least of it. Should Kienast once have done something good for somebody, something which, so to say, was in the general interest, he would have said coldheartedly, "Goodbye, *au revoir*," by which he meant to say, "Please leave me alone." He was interested only in personal gain, and he had eyes only for his supreme profit. Everything else concerned him little or preferably not at all. Of it he wanted to know absolutely nothing. Should anyone expect a willingness or even a sacrifice of him, he nasaled, "What next, I wonder?" by which he meant to say, "If you will be so kind as not to molest me with such matters." Or he said, "Remember me, please, it will make me happy," or very simply just, *"Bonsoir."* Community, church, and country seemed in no way to concern him. In his opinion, community affairs were looked after solely by jack-asses; whoever needed the church in any way was in Kienast's eyes a sheep, and for those who loved their country, he possessed not the least understanding. Tell me, dear readers, you who are aglow with patriotism for fatherland and motherland, what do you think should be done with the Kienasts? Wouldn't it be a splendid, yes even a sublime task to beat them in great haste and with the proper carefulness to a pulp? Gently! It has been seen to that such gentlemen will not remain eternally undisturbed. One day someone knocked at Kienast's door, someone who evidently did not allow himself to be turned away with a *"Bonjour"* or with a *"Bonsoir"* or with a "What next!" or with a "Sorry, I'm in a real hurry," or with a "Please leave me alone." "Come, I can use you," said the peculiar stranger. "You are really exquisite. But what's the matter with you? Do you think I have time to lose? That's the limit! Remember me, it will make me happy. Sorry I have no time, so goodbye, *au revoir."* Such or similar things Kienast wanted to answer; however, as he opened his mouth to say what he was thinking, he became sick to death, he was deathly pale, it was too late to say anything else, not one more word passed over his lips. It was Death who had come to him, it was all no use. Death makes its work brief. All his "Nonsenses" did no more good and all his beautiful *"Bonjours"* and *"Bonsoirs"* had an end. It was all over with scorn and mockery and with cold-heartedness. Oh, God, is such living a life? Would you like to live so lifelessly, so godlessly? To be so inhuman among human beings? Could someone cry out about you or about me if we had lived like Kienast? Could someone regret my death? Might it not be then that this or that person could almost be delighted about my departure?

[1917]

Translated by Tom Whalen and Carol Gehrig

Poets

To the question: How do authors of sketches, stories, and novels get along in life, the following answer can or must be given: They are stragglers and they are down at heel.

If thereupon it is seriously asked: Might there be exceptions?, then the reply is: Yes, there are exceptions, indeed there are, insofar as there exist, or seem to, writers who live in old country mansions, where, beside their proper tasks as authors, they do extensive and profitable business with milk, cattle, and grass. When evening comes, by the light of lamps they commit to paper their inspirations, either in their own handwriting, or else they dictate to their wives, or to a typist, so that nice clean copies may result. In this way entire exciting chapters come into being, which slowly but on the other hand surely expand into volumes, such as may eventually dominate the market.

If, again, it is asked: How and where, i.e., in what sorts of dwelling, do writers mostly live?, the answer is very simply this: It is a fact that they prefer to live, often, in attics, high up, with views all around, because from there they enjoy the broadest and freest outlook upon the world. They also like, as is well known, to be independent and unconstrained. Let us hope that they pay the rent, sometimes, as punctually as possible.

From experience I can say that poets, lyrical as well as epic and dramatic, very seldom heat their mathematical or philosophical rooms. "If you sweat all summer, you can freeze a bit for a change all winter," they say, and so they adjust, in a very talented manner, to both heat and cold. If, while they are sitting and writing, their legs, arms, and hands become stiff with cold, they need only to warm their fingers by breathing on them a while, or, in order to restore the lost suppleness of their joints, they can stand up and move their bodies about, this way and that, whereupon a sufficient quantum of warmth comes to them, of its own accord. Physical exercises are quite effective, what's more, in enlivening the mind, which may have been overworked and thus become slack. In general, creative energy, good thoughts, cheerful brainwaves, and the fiery poetic resolve can quite certainly, and at all times, be an almost perfect substitute for a glowing stove.

Yes, and I knew a poet, the author of most captivating verses, who lodged for a time in the bathroom of a lady, which tempts one to ask, if one may so ask, of course, whether or not he decently and promptly withdrew when the lady herself chose to take a bath.

Anyway, it is certain that this author felt uncommonly comfortable in the bathroom, which he decorated raffishly and romantically with old coats, fabrics, rags, and carpet remnants, and as far as is known, he maintained rigidly and stoutly that he was living in the Arabian style. Fantasy, ah, good heavens, what a nice, charming, and cheering creature she is.

We believe that writers are capable of polishing shoes as well as, or perhaps even better than, senators who dictate, or at least draft, a country's laws. The truth is that a senator once, i.e., in a good moment, confided to me that he polished, maintained, and cleaned his own shoes, as well as those of his beloved spouse, regularly and with the greatest pleasure. If leading senators have no hesitation, not the slightest, when it comes to the polishing of shoes, surely any writer of books, which have lasting value, may perform this task, which is a useful one, because it is extremely steadying for the nerves.

Are writers, next, to some extent competent in the removal of cobwebs? This question can be answered, without further detailed and time-wasting investigation, with a joyful affirmative. They can abolish a cobweb as nimbly as the most expert housemaid; in the mangling and destruction of such ingenious architectural monuments they are, quite simply, perfect barbarians, enjoying the task of demolition in the wickedest way, because it raises their spirits.

Every true poet likes dust, for it is in the dust, and in the most enchanting oblivion, that, as we all know, precisely the greatest poets like to lie, the classics, that is, whose fate is like that of old bottles of wine, which, to be sure, are drawn, only on particularly suitable occasions, out from under the dust and so exalted to a place of honor.

[1917]

Frau Wilke

O NE day, when I was looking for a suitable room, I entered
a curious house just outside the city and close to the
city tramway, an elegant, oldish, and seemingly rather neglected house, whose exterior had a singularity which at once
captivated me.

On the staircase, which I slowly mounted, and which was
wide and bright, were smells and sounds as of bygone elegance.

What they call former beauty is extraordinarily attractive to
some people. Ruins are rather touching. Before the residues of
noble things our pensive, sensitive inward selves involuntarily
bow. The remnants of what was once distinguished, refined,
and brilliant infuse us with compassion, but simultaneously
also with respect. Bygone days and old decrepitude, how enchanting you are!

On the door I read the name "Frau Wilke."

Here I gently and cautiously rang the bell. But when I
realized that it was no use ringing, since nobody answered, I
knocked, and then somebody approached.

Very guardedly and very slowly somebody opened the door.
A gaunt, thin, tall woman stood before me, and asked in a low
voice: "What is it you want?"

Her voice had a curiously dry and hoarse sound.

"May I see the room?"

"Yes, of course. Please come in."

The woman led me down a strangely dark corridor to the room, whose appearance immediately charmed and delighted me. Its shape was, as it were, refined and noble, a little narrow perhaps, yet proportionately tall. Not without a sort of irresolution, I asked the price, which was extremely moderate, so I took the room without more ado.

It made me glad to have done this, for a strange state of mind had much afflicted me for some time past, so I was unusually tired and longed to rest. Weary of all groping endeavor, depressed and out of sorts as I was, any acceptable security would have satisfied me, and the peace of a small resting place could not have been other than wholly welcome.

"What are you?" the lady asked.

"A poet!" I replied.

She went away without a word.

An earl, I think, might live here, I said to myself as I carefully examined my new home. This charming room, I said, proceeding with my soliloquy, unquestionably possesses a great advantage: it is very remote. It's quiet as a cavern here. Definitely: here I really feel I am concealed. My inmost want seems to have been gratified. The room, as I see it, or think I see it, is, so to speak, half dark. Dark brightness and bright darkness are floating everywhere. That is most commendable. Let's look around! Please don't put yourself out, sir! There's no hurry at all. Take just as much time as you like. The wallpaper seems, in parts, to be hanging in sad, mournful shreds from the wall. So it is! But that is precisely what pleases me, for I do like a certain degree of raggedness and neglect. The shreds can go on hanging; I'll not let them be removed at any price, for I am completely satisfied with them being there. I am much inclined to believe that a baron once lived here. Officers perhaps drank champagne here. The curtain by the window is tall and slender, it looks old and dusty; but being so prettily draped, it betokens good taste and reveals a delicate sensibility. Outside in the garden, close to the window, stands a birch tree. Here in summer the green will come laughing into the room, on the dear gentle branches all sorts of singing birds will gather, for their delight as well as for mine. This distinguished old writing table is wonderful, handed surely down from a past age of great acumen. Probably I shall write essays at it, sketches, studies, little stories, or even long stories, and send these, with urgent requests for quick and friendly publication, to all sorts of stern and highly reputable editors of papers and periodicals like, for example, *The Peking Daily News*, or *Mercure de France*, whence, for sure, prosperity and success must come.

The bed seems to be all right. In this case I will and must dispense with painstaking scrutiny. Then I saw, and here remark, a truly strange and ghostly hatstand, and the mirror there over the basin will tell me faithfully every day how I look. I hope the image it will give me to see will always be a flattering one. The couch is old, consequently pleasant and appropriate. New furniture easily disturbs one, because novelty is always importunate, always obstructs us. A Dutch and a Swiss landscape hang, as I observe to my glad satisfaction, modestly on the wall. Without a doubt, I shall look time and again at these two pictures most attentively. Regarding the air in this chamber, I would nevertheless deem it credible, or rather postulate at once with certitude almost, that for some time here no thought has been given to regular and, it seems, wholly requisite ventilation. I do declare that there is a smell of decay about the place. To inhale stale air provides a certain peculiar pleasure. In any case, I can leave the window open for days and weeks on end; then the right and good will stream into the room.

"You must get up earlier. I cannot allow you to stay in bed so long," Frau Wilke said to me. Beyond this, she did not say much.

This was because I spent entire days lying in bed.

I was in a bad way. Decrepitude surrounded me. I lay there as if in heaviness of heart; I neither knew nor could find myself any more. All my once lucid and gay thoughts floated in obscure confusion and disarray. My mind lay as if broken in fragments before my grieving eyes. The world of thought and of feeling was jumbled and chaotic. Everything dead, empty, and hopeless to the heart. No soul, no joy any more, and only faintly could I remember that there were times when I was happy and brave, kind and confident, full of faith and joy. The pity of it all! Before and behind me, and all around me, not the slightest prospect any more.

Yet I promised Frau Wilke to get up earlier, and in fact I did then also begin to work hard.

Often I walked in the neighboring forest of fir and pine, whose beauties, wonderful winter solitudes, seemed to protect me from the onset of despair. Ineffably kind voices spoke down to me from the trees: "You must not come to the dark conclusion that everything in the world is hard, false, and wicked. But come often to us; the forest likes you. In its company you will find health and good spirits again, and entertain more lofty and beautiful thoughts."

Into society, that is, where the big world foregathers, I never went. I had no business there, because I had no success. People who have no success with people have no business with people.

Poor Frau Wilke, soon afterwards you died.

Whoever has been poor and lonely himself understands other poor and lonely people all the better. At least we should learn to understand our fellow beings, for we are powerless to stop their misery, their ignominy, their suffering, their weakness, and their death.

One day Frau Wilke whispered, as she stretched out her hand and arm to me: "Hold my hand. It's like ice."

I took her poor, old, thin hand in mine. It was cold as ice.

Frau Wilke crept about her home now like a ghost. Nobody visited her. For days she sat alone in her unheated room.

To be alone: icy, iron terror, foretaste of the grave, forerunner of unpitying death. Oh, whoever has been himself alone can never find another's loneliness strange.

I began to realize that Frau Wilke had nothing to eat. The lady who owned the house, and later took Frau Wilke's rooms, allowing me to stay in mine, brought, of course in pity for her forsaken state, every midday and evening a cup of broth, but not for long, and so Frau Wilke faded away. She lay there, no longer moving: and soon she was taken to the city hospital, where, after three days, she died.

One afternoon soon after her death, I entered her empty room, into which the good evening sun was shining, gladdening it with rose-bright, gay and soft colors. There I saw on the bed the things which the poor lady had till recently worn, her dress, her hat, her sunshade and her umbrella, and, on the floor, her small delicate boots. The strange sight of them made me unspeakably sad, and my peculiar state of mind made it seem to me almost that I had died myself, and life in all its fullness, which had often appeared so huge and beautiful, was thin and poor to the point of breaking. All things past, all things vanishing away, were more close to me than ever. For a long time I looked at Frau Wilke's possessions, which now had lost their mistress and lost all purpose, and at the golden room, glorified by the smile of the evening sun, while I stood there motionless, not understanding anything any more. Yet, after standing there dumbly for a time, I was gratified and grew calm. Life took me by the shoulder and its wonderful gaze rested on mine. The world was as living as ever and beautiful as at the most beautiful times. I quietly left the room and went out into the street.

[1918]

The Street (1)

I HAD taken some steps, useless they had been, and now I went out into the street, agitated, numb. At first it was like being sightless, and I thought nobody saw anybody any more, everybody had been blinded and life was at a standstill, everybody groping around in confusion.

Because my nerves were so tense, I sensed things with exceptional sharpness. Façades rose up before me, cold. Heads and clothes rushed towards me and vanished like ghosts.

A shiver passed through me; I hardly dared to walk on. One impression after another seized hold of me. I was swaying, everything was swaying. All the people walking here had plans in mind, business. A moment before, I too had had an end in view; but now, no plans at all, but I was searching for one again, and I hoped to find something.

The crowds were seething with energy. Everybody thought himself out in front. Men, women floated by. All seemed to be making for the same goal. Where did they come from, where were they going?

One of them was this, another that, a third nothing. Many were driven, lived without purpose, let themselves be flung every which way. Any sense for the good was set aside, not used; intelligence was groping in emptiness; fine faculties and plenty bore meager fruit.

Evening had come; the street was like an apparition. Thousands walked here every day. There was no room anywhere else. Early in the morning they were brisk; at night, tired. Often they came to nothing. Actions rolled over one another; ability was often exasperated, to no end.

As I was walking along thus, I met the gaze of a grandee's coachman. Then I jumped onto a bus, rode on for a stretch, went into a restaurant to eat something, and then I went out again. Everywhere an even-measured going and flowing. Human understanding was taken for granted. Everyone knew, in an instant, pretty well everything about everyone else, but the interior life remained secret. Soul continuously renews itself.

Wheels were grinding, voices became loud; yet the whole scene was oddly still.

I wanted to speak with someone, but found no time; sought some fixed point, but found none. In the midst of the unrelenting forward thrust I felt the wish to stand still. The muchness and the motion were too much and too fast. Everyone withdrew from everyone. There was a running, as of something liquefied, a constant going forth, as of evaporation. Everything was schematic, ghostlike, even myself.

Suddenly I saw an unspeakable heaviness in all the haste and hurry, and I told myself: "This hugger-mugger totality wants nothing and does nothing. They are entangled with one another, do not move, prisoners; they abandon themselves to opaque pressures but they themselves are the power that lies upon them and binds them, mind and limb."

As I was passing by, a woman's eyes spoke to me: "Come with me. Quit the whirlpool, leave that farrago behind, join the only person who will make you strong. If you are loyal to me, you'll be rich. In the turmoil you are poor."

I wanted to follow her call, but was swept away in the stream. The street was just too irresistible.

Then I came into the open country, where everything was

quiet. A train with red windows hurtled past, close by. In the distance the traffic's billowing ceaseless subtle thunder was faintly to be heard.

I walked along the edge of the forest and murmured a poem by Brentano. The moon was glancing through the branches.

Suddenly I noticed a man standing not far off, quite motionless, and apparently watching for me.

I walked around him, keeping him constantly in sight, which annoyed him; for he called out to me: "Why not come here and take a proper look at me? I am not what you think."

I went over to him. He was like anyone else, except that he looked strange, nothing more. Then I went back again to where the light was, and the street.

[1919]

Snowdrops

I've just been writing a letter in which I announced that I had
finished a novel with or without pain and distress, that the
considerable manuscript was lying in my drawer ready to go,
with the title already in position and packing paper at hand,
for the work to be wrapped and sent in. Furthermore, I have
purchased a new hat, which for the present I shall wear only
on Sundays, or when a visitor comes to me.

Recently a parson visited me. I found it nice and most proper
that he did not look at all like a professional one. The parson
told me of a lyrically gifted teacher. I intend to go before long
on foot through the spring country to this person, who instructs
the village schoolchildren and writes verse as well. I find it
beautiful and natural that a teacher should concern himself
with higher things and have experiences of the more profound
sort. Yet on account of his profession he has to deal with something serious: with souls! Here I think of the wonderful *Life of
the Merry Schoolmaster, Maria Wuz, of Auenthal, a Kind of
Idyll*, by Jean Paul, a book, or booklet, that I have read with delight I know not how often and will probably read again and
again. The main point is that now the spring is just beginning
again. So here and there I'll succeed in writing a pleasant-
sounding line of springtime verse. It is wonderful that now one

need not think at all of heating. Thick winter coats will soon
have outplayed their role. Everybody will be glad if he can
stand around and go about coatless. Thank God there are still
things about which everyone is united and agrees nicely with
one another.

I have seen snowdrops; in gardens and on the cart of a
peasant woman who was driving to market. I wanted to buy a
bouquet from her, but thought it not right for a robust man
like me to ask for so tender a thing. They are sweet, these first
shy announcers of something beloved by all the world. Everyone loves the thought that it will become spring.

It is all a folk play, and the entry costs not a penny. Nature,
the sky above us, is conducting no mean politics when it presents beauty to all, without discrimination, and nothing old and
defective, but fresh and most tasty. Little snowdrops, of what
do you speak? They speak still of winter, but also already of
spring; they speak of the past, but also saucily and merrily of
the new. They speak of the cold but also of something warmer;
they speak of snow and at the same time of green, of burgeon-
ing growth. They speak of this and that; they say: Still in the
shadows and on the hills lies a fair quantity of snow, but where
the sun reaches, it has already melted away. Yet all sorts of
hoarfrost may still come this way. April is not to be trusted.
But what we wish will nevertheless win out. The warmth will
assert itself everywhere.

Snowdrops whisper all kinds of things. They bring back to
mind Snow White, who in the mountains found a friendly welcome from the dwarfs. They remind one of roses because they
are different. Everything always reminds one of its opposite.

Just wait. The good will come. Goodness is always closer to
us than we think. Patience brings roses. This old, good saying
occurred to me when recently I saw snowdrops.

[1919]

Translated by Tom Whalen and Trudi Anderegg

Winter

IN winter the fog makes much of itself. Anyone walking in it cannot help but shiver. Only seldom does the sun honor us with its presence. Then one feels somewhat reprieved, as by the entrance of a beautiful woman who knows how to make herself delectable.

Winter excels with cold. It is to be hoped that all rooms are heated, all overcoats worn. Furs and slippers increase in importance, fire in attraction, warmth in demand. Winter has long nights, short days, and bare trees. Not one green leaf appears now. But ice appears, on lakes and rivers, and in its wake something very pleasant; namely, skating. If snow falls, snowball fights are likely. These are a children's pastime; an adult prefers to smoke cigars, sit at a table, and play cards, or else adults fancy serious conversation. Sledding might also be mentioned, by the way, an activity pleasing to many.

Glorious sunny winter days there are. Footsteps clink over frozen ground. If there is snow, everything is soft, it's as if you were walking on a carpet. Snowy landscapes have a beauty all their own. Everything looks festive, as for a ceremony. Christmastime is especially delightful for children. Then the Christmas tree shines brightly, or rather, the candles, which fill the room with a radiance devout and beautiful. How enchanting!

The fir-tree branches are hung with delicacies. These are, in particular, chocolate angels, candy cippolatas, biscuits from Basel, walnuts wrapped in silver foil, red-cheeked apples. Around the tree the members of the family are gathered. The children recite poems they have learned by heart. Afterwards their parents show them their presents, and say to them something like: "Be as good a child as you have been till now," and they kiss the children, whereupon the children kiss the parents, and perhaps all of them, amid such beautiful circumstances and deeply felt things, weep for a while and say thank you to each other in trembling voices, and hardly know why they are doing so, though they think it is right, and are happy. See how in the middle of winter love is radiant, brightness smiles, warmth shines, tenderness twinkles, and the glow of all that may be hoped for, all kindness, comes toward you.

Snow does not fall lickety-split, but slowly, that is, bit by bit, which means flake by flake, down to the earth. Everything is flying around, as in Paris, where it does not snow as it does, for instance, in Moscow, from where Napoleon once began his retreat, because he thought it was advisable. It snows in London too, where Shakespeare once lived, who wrote *The Winter's Tale*, a play glittering with merriment and gravity, in equal measure, in which a reunion occurs, attended by one of the characters, who stands by like a "conduit of many kings' reigns," as it says in the text.

Isn't snowfall an enchanting spectacle? To be snowed in, once in a while, certainly does no great harm. Years ago I experienced a snowstorm on the Friedrichstrasse in Berlin, and it is still vivid in my memory.

Recently I dreamed I flew over a round, fragile sheet of ice, as thin and transparent as a windowpane, and curving up and down like glassy waves. Beneath the ice, spring flowers were growing. As if raised up by a spirit, I floated back and forth and was pleased by the effortless motion. In the middle of the lake was an island on which stood a temple which turned out to be a tavern. I went in, ordered coffee and cakes, and ate and drank and afterward smoked a cigarette. When I left and resumed my exercise, the mirror broke and I sank into the depths, among the flowers, which admitted me with a friendly welcome.

How nice it is that spring follows winter, every time.

[1919]

The She-Owl

A SHE-OWL in a ruined wall said to herself: What a horrifying existence. Anyone else would be dismayed, but me, I am patient. I lower my eyes, huddle. Everything in me and on me hangs down like gray veils, but above me, too, the stars glitter; this knowledge fortifies me. Bushy plumage covers me: by day I sleep, at night I'm awake. I need no mirror to discover how I look: feeling tells me. I can easily think of my peculiar face.

People say I'm ugly. If they only knew what smiles I feel in my soul, they'd not run from me in fright any more. Yet they don't see into the interior, they stop at the body, the clothes. Once I was young and pretty, I might say, but that makes it sound as if I pine for the past, and that is not my way. The she-owl, who once practiced growing big, endures the course and change of time tranquilly, she finds herself in every present moment.

They say to me: "Philosophy." Yet the death that comes beforetimes cancels the later one. Death is nothing new to the she-owl, she knows it already. It looks as if I'm a lady of learning, wear glasses, and somebody is so interested in me that he pays me a visit now and then. He finds me Harmonious. He tells me I'm somebody who doesn't disappoint him. Of course, I have never bewitched him either. He studies me profoundly, strokes my wings, brings me candy sometimes, with which to delight, so he believes, the most serious of females, and he's making no mistake. I am reading a poet whose finesse makes him fit to be digested by owls. There's something sweet in his ways, something veiled, undefinable, which is to say, he suits me well. Once I was charming, I laughed and twittered jokes into the blue of day, I turned many young men's heads. Now things look different, the shoes I wear have holes in them, I'm old, I sit and say nothing.

[1921]

Knocking

I AM completely beat, this head hurts me.

Yesterday, the day before yesterday, the day before the day before yesterday, my landlady knocked.

"May I know why you are knocking?" I asked her.

This timid question was turned down with the response: "You are pretentious."

Subtle questions are perceived as impertinent.

One should always make a lot of noise.

Knocking is a true pleasure, listening to it less so. Knockers don't hear their knocking; i.e., they hear it, but it doesn't disturb them. Each thump has something agreeable for the originator. I know that from my own experience. One believes oneself brave when making a racket.

There's that knocking again.

Apparently it's a rug being worked on. I envy all those who, thrashing, exercise harmlessly.

An instructor once took several students over his knee and spanked them thoroughly, to impress upon them that bars exist only for adults. I also was among the group beneficially beaten.

Anyone who wants to hang a picture on the wall must first pound in a nail. To this end, one must knock.

"Your knocking disturbs me."

"That doesn't concern me."

"Good, then I shall compliantly see to the removal of this irritation."

"It won't hurt you."

A polite conversation, don't you agree?

Knocking, knocking! I'd like to stop up my ears.

Also, I once dusted as a servant the Persian carpets for the household of a count. The sound of it echoed through the magnificent landscape.

Clothes, mattresses, etc., are beaten.

So a modern city is full of knocking. Anyone who worries over something inevitable seems a simpleton.

"Go ahead, knock as much as you like."

"Is that meant ironically?"

"Yes, a little."

[1923]

Translated by Tom Whalen and Carol Gehrig

Titus

Doesn't it sound like sheer swank to bring to these lips, Titus narrated, that my mother was a princess, and that bandits kidnapped me in order to make me one of them? I say that only for the sake of ornamentation, so that you won't be bored with me from the very beginning. If someone asked me about my birthplace, I would declare it was Goslar, though with that I would be telling a juicy lie. Never was I spoiled by my mother, for which I should be only too pleased. Goslar, so I read some time ago, is enchanting in its spring raiment, and since I tend to be a trusting soul, I readily accepted the assertion. While with the robbers, I learned to wash, sew, cook, and play Chopin, but I would like to request that you not take this statement too strictly. It seems to me like I am properly fantasizing here, for which I should be granted indulgence. Should the poet not be allowed to play as freely upon the instrument of his imagination as, for example, a musician on the piano? As a lieutenant I had a servant who spoiled me. I came to a city, went through the streets, and searched and found an appropriate job, obtained room and board with a family, whose head was as surly as his wife was indulgent. I taught both their boys the art of cigarette rolling and learned English in the company of a young woman. Tall and pale,

like a breathed-upon rose from romanticism, sat, kindhearted-
ness in her eyes, a waitress in her room; she made me, with two
words which she did not begrudge me, happy, even though I
did not yet rightly know the meaning of bliss. A third tenant, a
widow, got so familiar with me that the grumbly one announced that he could not sanction such flirtations in his dwelling. Peace is a difficult problem. I took to writing only to give it
up little by little. To the east of an enormous shopping district,
I met in a bar a dark-eyed girl enveloped in yellow. Doesn't
that, however, sound like rummaging up memories and
couldn't it easily have the effect of sentimentality in print? For
a mediocre type like me it was the same as for those whose
main experience is to pass many people by without making
contact with them. I am unusual perhaps only in that I lost
terribly much time and perceived this fact with pleasure. Instead of older, I grew younger. That I became a bit duller is
something I definitely take pride in. I am proud and narrow-
minded and I tugged about on my nose so persistently it obtained a charming form, prayed constantly to the dear Lord for
a childish appearance, which I also succeeded in getting. My
heart is a snake's nest, it's no wonder whenever I raise my eyes
pleadingly to people who for that reason think me docile, but
what kind of sentence-disfiguring improprieties are these! He
who does not have the good intention to tell a lie is hopelessly
lost. Honesty is seldom respectable. I have a confession to
make, I carry about a love that partly troubles me, but that
also gives me wings. Required by a cooperative for the promo-
tion of poetry to deliver a new manuscript, I hied, wagged, and
ran my way into every coffeehouse where a lady seemed con-
descending enough to allow me to look up to her. Since then I
am both the palest and most ruddy devotee. It's just a pity that
Solomonian songs of love have already been written and exist
in the books at hand; how gladly would I steal through the
servant's entrance into the palaces of literature and serve with
rapture. Yesterday I went to the country, which was dressed in
a kind of early-spring gold, took off my hat to sweet Mama
Nature, sat down on a small bench, and cried. In the multiple

branching network of the methods of rejuvenescence, tears are, to my experience, a not unimportant point of intersection. People no longer let their fingernails grow. The opposite kind thinks about marriage. Hair must be washed every week. The waves amused themselves at my feet, and throughout the valley, which consisted of gentle hills gently following one another, there was a serenity like that cast in the face of a man who has remained good, who has lived for years without life turning him to disfavor. The oldness and youthfulness of the earth are wonderful. With your permission, I shall speak and sing about a small dancing brook falling down a wall of rock, sparkling silver, laughing and divinely beautiful, solemn and merry as it splashed on the rocks, broke away as a small contribution to the colossus ocean, where in thousand-fathom depths innocent monsters swim eternally around wet and hidden trees, luxury liners decorate the surface, and I shall talk about soft shadows on the meadow, small houses on the incline, and a youth lying down. It would be dreadful if the reader just yawned! With a languishing soul and with eyes opened wide like circles from yearning, I went into a peaceful garden where the sun faintly shone through, listened to the orchestra giving a sympathetic concert here, whereby I apparently behaved bizarrely because out of pity a girl fell over in a death of daggerlike piercing regrets; whoever thinks this possible will be happy for the rest of his life. I let people who take to me build on the structure of their friendship as long as they wish; they never become bothered by me because I notice them not at all. Many incautiously take me to be uncivilized. My most exalted is so beautiful and I worship her with such a holy respect that I attach myself to another and therewith must seize the opportunity to recover from the strain of sleepless nights, to relate to the successor how dear the past one was, to tell her, "I love you just as much."

[1925]

Translated by Tom Whalen and Carol Gehrig

Vladimir

WE shall call him Vladimir, since it is a rare name and in point of fact he was unique. Those to whom he appeared foolish tried to win a glance, a word from him, which he rarely gave. In inferior clothes he behaved more sanguinely than in elegant ones, and was basically a good person who merely made the mistake of falsely attributing and affixing to himself faults which he did not have. He was hard primarily on himself. Isn't that inexcusable?

Once he lived with a married couple and was impossible to drive away. "It is time that you left us alone," was intimated to him; he seemed hardly able to imagine it, saw the woman smiling and the man turn pale. He was chivalry itself. Serving always gave him a lofty notion of the bliss of existence. He could not see pretty women burdened with small boxes, packages, and so on, without springing forth and expressing the wish to be helpful, at which he first always fought back the slightest fear of intruding.

From whence did Vladimir descend? Well, certainly from none other than his parents. It seems peculiar that he admits when down on his luck to having often been happy, when successful to having been morose, and that he says the driving force of his existence is his industriousness. No one ever saw such a satisfied and at the same time dissatisfied man. No one was quicker and in the very next instant more irresolute.

Once a girl promised to meet him at such and such a time and then kept him waiting. This came as a surprise to him. Another asserted, "It befits you to be swindled. Do you not have a peculiar predilection for jokes which border on disregard?"

"You are mistaken," is all he answered.

He never bore a person a grudge, because "I, too, have often played unfairly with people."

At the ladies' café he was amused by the mimicry and expressions of the customers. By the way, he was no friend of too many diversions, as much as he valued them by way of exception. He thought about everything only to forget it in an instant, was a good reckoner because he did not permit his feelings to have power over his mind.

The women thought little of him, but not without always becoming interested in him again. They called him timid, but he likewise them. They played with and feared him.

To one lady, who flaunted her wealth before him in perhaps too clever a manner, he was most courteous, as one is when one feels for that person nothing. He found uncultured girls inspired by their need for instruction and on the other hand also such who have read everything and now wished to be almost ignorant. For injustices suffered he never avenged himself and perhaps avenged himself sufficiently in just this way. Those who did not treat him as he had wished, he let go, dropped; that is to say, he accustomed himself to not thinking about many unpleasant things. That's how he protected his soul from confusion, his thoughts from unhealthy hardness.

Music put him in a tender mood, as it does most people. If he saw himself favored by a girl, it seemed as if she wished to hold him down, and he kept clear of her. He was as suspicious as a southerner, of himself as well as others; frequently jealous but never for long, because his self-respect quickly freed him from the persecution of envy, envy which to him seemed hardly awakened, unfounded, and of no substance.

Once he lost a friend, and said to himself, "He's losing as much as I." He worshipped a woman until she made one error, and it was no longer possible for him to pine for her. A rash remark from her had the result that he laughed at her, and he was happy about it. Feeling sorry for her, he no longer needed to be sorry for himself.

He stayed young and used his strength for the acquiring and exercise of attention to people who most needed not to be glanced over insensitively, the feeble and the aged. Do we speak too highly of him?

Sometimes he carries on like a gad-about-town, visits so-called vulgar dives. There are people around who rebuke him for it, but who would themselves gladly be mirthful, which their spheres so seldom allow. He has had imitators, but the original remains himself. Imitation, by the way, is quite natural.

Copies can also be appealing, but only from the original can great value come.

[1925]

Translated by Tom Whalen and Carol Gehrig

Parisian Newspapers

Since I have been reading the Parisian papers, from which the scent of power emanates, I have become so refined that I do not return greetings and, what's more, this amazes me not at all. With *Le Temps* in my hand, I appear very elegant to myself. Furthermore, I will no longer even glance at righteous people. To me the Parisian papers are a substitute for the theater. Also, not even the finest restaurant will I honor with my feet, so subtle have I become. Gulps of beer no longer pass my lips. My ear approves only of the melodiousness of the French language. Once I adored a lady, a true lady; today I find her most clumsy, since *Le Figaro* has spoiled me. Did *Le Matin* not drive me half mad? While my colleagues write themselves sick in this modern time of crisis, I grow exuberant through my papers. A trip which I intended to take to Paris I consider completed, I become acquainted with France's capital by way of reading. It is pleasing to be in good company. The papers of conquerors make the best society. German language products get no more blessings from me. I have forgotten how to speak German; I wonder if there is any harm in that?

[1925]

Translated by Tom Whalen and Carol Gehrig

The Monkey

TENDERLY yet in some degree hardheartedly should this tale be tackled, which declares that it occurred to a monkey one afternoon to drop into a coffeehouse and idle away the time of day there. Upon his decidedly not unintelligent head he was wearing a hard hat, or it may even have been a slouch hat, and on his hands the most elegant gloves that were ever displayed in a fashion shop for gentlemen. His suit was superb. With one or two curiously executed, featherweight, really remarkable, though slightly revealing leaps he arrived in the tearoom, through which rustled, like whisperings of foliage, an enticing music. The monkey was at a loss regarding where he should sit, in a modest corner, or slap in the middle. He chose the latter since it dawned on him that monkeys, if they behave with decorum, may after all appear in public. Melancholically but also glad, unperturbed and at the same time bashfully, he looked about him, discovering many a pretty maid's little face, with lips as of cherry juice and with cheeks as of pure whipped or clotted cream. Beautiful eyes and mellifluous melodies were striving for mastery, and I faint with narrative pride and wonder to report that the monkey, speaking the vernacular, asked the waitress who served him whether he might be permitted to scratch? "Of course, if you want to," she kindly replied, and our cavalier, if he merits the title, made such extensive use of her permission that ladies present partly laughed, partly looked aside so as not to have to join the others in looking at what he made so bold as to do. When an evidently charming woman sat down at his table, he began immediately to entertain her with great wit; he spoke about the weather, and then about books. "What an extraordinary person!" she mused, as he tossed his gloves into the air and deftly caught them again. He curled his lips into an enchanting grimace when he smoked. His cigarette provided a most lively contrast with his austere complexion.

Preziosa was the name of the young lady who now entered the room, like a romance, or a ballade, accompanied by a pomelo of an aunt, and from this moment there was no more peace for the monkey, who had never known before what it is to love. He knew it now. Suddenly all the nonsense was swept out of his head. With resolute step he approached his heart's elect and desired her to become his wife; he knew a trick or two to show her what sort of a person he was! The young lady said: "You shall come home with us. I must say you are hardly suitable for a husband. If you behave well, you will receive every day a tap on the nose. You are radiant! I'll allow you that. You will see to it that I do not get bored." So saying, she rose up so proudly that a roar of laughter came over the monkey, whereupon she boxed his ears.

When they got home, the Jewess sat down, having dismissed her aunt with a gesture, upon an expensive golden-footed sofa, and asked the monkey, who was standing before her in picturesque pose, to tell her who he was, to which this quintessence of monkeyhood answered:

"I once wrote poems on the Zürichberg; these I now submit in print to the object of my devotions. Though your eyes attempt to crush me to the floor, which is impossible, for the sight of you raises me continually up again, formerly indeed I often went into the forest to my lady friends, the pines, looked up at their crests, lay full length on the moss, till I grew weary from my sprightliness, and melancholy from gladness—"

"You lazy thing!" interjected Preziosa.

The family friend, for as such he already ventured to consider himself, continued, and said: "Once I left a dentist's bill unpaid, believing I would nevertheless succeed in life, and I sat at the feet of women of higher society, who accorded me a quantum of benevolence. Then you might also be informed that in autumn I picked windfall apples, gathered flowers in spring, and for a season lived where a poet named Keller grew up, of whom you will probably not have heard, although you ought to have done—"

"Impudence!" the young lady cried. "It would give me the greatest of pleasure to dismiss you, only to grieve you; still, I'll be merciful. But if you are ever ungallant again, you will have breathed in my presence for the last time, long for me as you may. Now, proceed."

He began again, and said: "I never gave much to women, and so they value me. Also in you, miss, I detect an admiration for the simplest loon ever to utter indiscretions to ladies merely to make them angry and afterwards content again. I arrived as ambassador in Constantinople—"

"No lies, Mr. Braggart!"

"—and one day at the railway terminus caught sight of a lady-in-waiting, that is to say, another person saw her, I was sitting next to him in the carriage, he reported to me the observation which I now dish up to you, though only figuratively, for there's no dish, howbeit I long for a loaded one, because I have developed an appetite in presenting to you a specimen of my powers of rhetoric."

"Go into the kitchen and serve supper. Meanwhile, I shall read your verses."

He did as he was told, went into the kitchen, but could not find it. Did he go into it without even having set eyes on it? There must have been a slight slip of the pen.

He went back to Preziosa, who had fallen asleep over his poems, who lay there like a picture in an Oriental fairy tale. One of her hands hung down like a cluster of grapes. He wanted to tell her how he had gone into the kitchen without having found where it was, how gradually, gradually he had grown silent, but an irrefragable impulse had driven him back to the lady he had abandoned. He stood before the sleeper, knelt at the shrine of loveliness, and touched the hand that seemed to him like a Jesukin, too beautiful to hold, with his breath alone.

While he was making his reverences—which one would hardly have expected of him—her eyes opened. She had a lot of questions to ask him, but she only said: "You do not seem to me to be a proper monkey at all. Tell me, are you a royalist?"

"Why should I be that?"

"Because you are so patient, and you spoke of ladies-in-waiting."

"I only want to be polite."

"It appears that is just what you are."

The next day she wanted him to tell her how to find happiness. He gave her the most astonishing answer. "Come, I'll dictate you a letter," she said. While he was writing, she glanced over his shoulder to see if he was taking it all faithfully down. Phew! How nimbly he wrote, listening with the most pointed attention to every syllable she spoke. We leave them to their correspondence.

In the birdcage pranced a cockatoo.

Preziosa was thinking of something.

[1925]

Dostoevsky's "Idiot"

THE contents of Dostoevsky's *Idiot* pursue me. Lapdogs interest me greatly. I'm not searching for someone as lively as an Aglaya. Unfortunately, she would, of course, take someone else. Marie remains unforgettable to me. One morning did I not stop and stand affectionately before a jackass? Who will introduce me to a General Epanchin's wife? Valets have wondered about me already, too. It is still questionable whether or not I write as nicely as the offspring of the house of Myshkin and whether or not I have inherited millions. It would be splendid to be taken into the confidence of a beautiful woman. Why haven't I yet seen a merchant's house like that of Rogozhin? Why don't I suffer from convulsive seizures? The idiot was thin, made only a poor impression. A good lad, at whose feet the demimondaine knelt one evening. I definitely expect something similar. I know two or three Kolyas. Wouldn't an Ivolgin also have to be seen? I'd be capable of knocking down a vase: to doubt this would be to underrate oneself. To make a speech is as difficult as it is easy; it depends on inspiration. I've often encountered people who are never satisfied with themselves. Often enough a person is not well because he tries too hard to be pleased with himself. Thereafter I'd arrive in the Schneider Institute. For the time being,

Nastasia would have to be pacified. I'm by no means idiotic, but am receptive to every reasonable thing; I'm sorry I'm not the hero of a novel. I'm not up to playing such a part, I just read a lot sometimes.

[1925]

Translated by Tom Whelan and Carol Gehrig

Am I Demanding?

PEOPLE draw my attention to novels by important authors.
I receive letters from publishers.

Society women are mindful of me.

I have genteel manners; of course I suddenly discard them, and then later recover them.

Sometimes I do think I'm odd.

Doctors ask me, in all sympathy, if it's really true that nobody cares for me, as if they thought it very incorrect.

Soon even I'll be believing I've been neglected. Yet there's no harm in that, none at all. On the contrary, because of it, I have "lived" that much more intensely.

Every noon, at lunch, I read "my" newspaper. This fact asks to be mentioned. Is there anything else out there asking for a friendly announcement from me?

Could I have "forgotten all sorts of things"?

Once more I've changed my domicile. When shall I get around to reading a French book again? I'm longing to do so.

What does "being cultivated" mean? What are all these questions I'm asking myself?

I like looking for a room and that sort of thing. You can look into houses which you would otherwise not look into.

Thus, for instance, while searching for a suitable working

space and living room, I arrived inside a house from the baroque period. Old pictures were hanging in the corridors.

Needless to say, I remain interested primarily in attics. I'm interested in so many things.

Shall I soon apply politely for a job? This question, too, weighs enormously on my mind.

In the house of some quite poor people I found a very nice room, but it could not, unfortunately, be heated. At once I declared myself agreeable to the view across the countryside afforded by the tiny window. The room could only be regarded as a sort of cubbyhole.

While looking at this room I was also looking at the landlady. I wanted to find out if she might conceivably become more "intimately" interesting to me.

Moreover, in the little window, standing at some distance on a hill, you could see a People's Nutrition Building, in which questions of economics and management could be studied. In this elegant house a professor of literature and art once used to live. Somebody had told me this, and now I thought of it. A woman of my acquaintance works there, as a janitress; I met her when she was the keeper of a boardinghouse.

"The table is a bit too small for me, you see I write rather a lot," I said to the landlady, whose appearance I had scrutinized. I said goodbye to her and went away.

Later I looked at a dark but warm room on a courtyard. To the woman who showed it to me, I said: "Perhaps I'll come back. At the moment I'm pierced through with arrows."

"For heaven's sake," she asked, dismayed, "what kind of arrows?"

"Cupid's arrows," I replied calmly, and most casually, as if these arrows were really no business of mine.

"Yes, some women give no mercy," she added. I answered: "It's understandable, every woman's first concern is herself."

Whereupon I left, and now this very peculiar question, in my opinion an important one, occupies my thoughts: "Of what does being cultivated consist?" And then this second question, a most important one, it too gives me no peace, the question, I mean, as to what the People means. How on earth shall I cope with these problems?

And this doctor who, in an offhand sort of way, as it were, briefly "mothered" me. He gave me a book to read, which now graces my desk with its presence.

And then "this beautiful woman," who gazes at me in a shop, so intently, as if she wanted to tell me: "I know you; watch out!"

She had such a beautiful, delicate face, also very delicate feet. The thing was this: I was just sitting there in the shop waiting for something. Of this woman I at once thought I had met her somewhere before, that she recognized me, and that she had a quite definite opinion of me. Of course, all this might have been a delusion of mine. One is so easily deluded about the objects of one's interest.

Early in the morning, one sees in our nicest of towns numerous pretty girls who are on the way to some occupation or other.

It's gradually becoming "serious," my situation, I realize this.

I've decided to write a novel, which will have to be psychological, of course. It will be concerned with vital questions.

A schoolteacher, who is also an author, has written me two very attentive, intelligent letters.

Oh, this rapidity in all my prolonged slownesses, and, on the other hand, this sloth again, in all my extensive industriousness.

Is it really the case that I'm a kind of child of the people, who doesn't yet understand even himself? That would be terrible.

But I always float, like the price of gold, that's to say, modestly put, I have confidence in myself. Others, alas, do not, not always, as, for instance, a very nice woman, to whom I also spoke while looking for a room.

The room looked captivating, you know, so sunny, so bright. I told myself at once: "I'd like to live here." The wash table was new and snow-white, and there was an inviting chaise longue, which I would have placed otherwise, probably.

"The room is a real poem, dear esteemed lady," said I to the person who wanted to rent it. "In spirit I have settled down here already."

She answered: "I must tell you, to my own regret and probably to yours as well, that I cannot make a decision at once. You are very demanding, aren't you?"

I replied: "Yes, I am."

"For that reason I must ask you to give me a little time for reflection. Telephone me, will you? Won't you? Then I'll tell you."

I took leave of that marvel of a room. How I laugh, when I think about it now! And about the woman who sought salvation in delay.

As for me, I now live in a decent place, it's almost refined. My surroundings satisfy me. One can live pretty well anywhere, I believe, and what's more, somebody who knows and thinks well of me, a person of importance in the business line, has been asking after my modest self, and I believe, she will have obtained the information she wanted.

I think I still have it in me to make something of myself. And I'd like to add: an actress has written to me, saying how she arrived home in a troubled mood, thought of me, and the thought made her happy.

[1925]

The Little Tree

I SEE it, even when I walk past, hardly noticing. It does not run away, stands quite still, cannot think, cannot desire anything, no, it can only grow, be, in space, and have leaves, which nobody touches, which are only to be looked at. Busy people hurry on past the shadow offered by the leaves.

Have I never given anything to you? Yet it needs no happiness. Perhaps, if someone thinks it is beautiful, it is glad. Do you think so? What holy innocences speak from it. It knows of nothing; it is there for my pleasure, that only.

Why can it not be sensitive to my love, when I say something to it, the good thing? But it apprehends nothing. It never sees me when I smile at the greeting it ignorantly gives.

To die at this being's feet, like that figure Courbet painted, who is taking leave forever.

Surely I shall go on living, but what will become of you?

[1925]

Stork and Hedgehog

HEDGEHOG: Aren't I captivating? Tell me!

STORK: For a long time I have loved you.

HEDGEHOG: I'll say nothing about that. I don't talk to creatures that love me. Love is something so reckless, impudent! I'll have no dealings with spendthrifts. Make a note of that. It's my spines you're in love with, isn't it?

STORK: Your mantle of spines suits you charmingly. You look adorable in it. A pity you're so prudish. A hedgehog should not be so buttoned up about decent behavior.

HEDGEHOG: You're wrong, and I'll tell you something. A stork can brag of many things, but a hedgehog can't. You are flattered, you are an educational and family ideal. Whole communities look up to you with unfeigned respect. All the opinions that go with you are good ones. With me, it's different. What use to me is your affection? Have you been smitten by my timorousness?

STORK: Yes, I think so.

HEDGEHOG: It suits me fine, don't you think? I'm so nice and round in it, so appetizing. I have spines because I'm afraid. I am all flight and fear. Look at my little head, my little eyes, my little nose. I don't fly, with majesty, like you. There's not a tittle of elevation about me. My feet are incomprehensibility itself, but I am dainty, I look like some poor silly thing. I don't strut about with wings, not likely. I don't build, on church steeples, comfortable nests with the bright air wafting around them. I live in forests, only venture forth, softly, in the dark.

STORK: You dear shy thing!

HEDGEHOG: You take pity on me. But I have no pity. Pity is something grand. It doesn't suit me. I am puny. My spines, what's more, are mockery itself; they mock me.

STORK: So you're mocked by what seems called upon to shield you. I love you all the more for your forsakenness.

HEDGEHOG: But I'm in enormously good spirits. You have no idea how splendidly one can live inside a covering that's laughable. My well-being is unspeakably original. The assurance that I look pretty streams through me, it fairly does. You're rather a comical one yourself.

STORK: My dignity, you mean. But I can't do anything about it. I appear somewhat stiff, solemn, but it's precisely in this gravity of my manner that I myself vanish, do you understand?

HEDGEHOG: I don't allow myself to understand anything. Understanding would annoy me. Do you think I'd take the trouble to start looking into you? Deep thinking I leave to you and your kind. I'm sorry for you because you can't put me out of your mind, but I find it funny that you make me feel sorry for you. So then I'm not really sorry for you at all. Look, I'm shaped like a hill and give an impression of lifelessness.

STORK: That's a huge advantage. I admire you, are you giggling at something?

HEDGEHOG: Oh, only at the anxieties of such an intelligence as yours. To be cultivated and want to extract a smile from a hedgehog! Inner glee is all I feel. On the outside I would never laugh. I mind my good manners too much for that. Besides, I've been talking with you for too long. You love me. But me, feathered friend, me you fill with horror. Yet I only shrink from you because that happens to suit me. Shrinking, I find, is my pleasure.

STORK: Do you despise me?

HEDGEHOG: My spines tell me I should. Otherwise, you'd impress me. But you're also much too long-leggity, big-beaked, too proud, too beautiful for me.

STORK: Would that your inconspicuousness could be the death of me.

The hedgehog tucks himself entirely into his mantle, still peering out a little. Sees the good stork trembling with his inclination, swathed in his slendernesses. But he speaks no more. Finds speech from now on pointless; simply crouches there still, unspeakably odd and incomprehensible. The stork stands transfixed. Hedgehoggish helplessness invades him. Deep down, the hedgehog is a complete child, and, loving what is solitary, the kindly stork is now himself strange and solitary. He thinks that he too is tricked out with spines. Night has fallen in the forest; the enchanted stork stands on one leg, plunged in a lofty sorrow of love.

The hedgehog ignores him.

Apparently the hedgehog is asleep.

But that is not so. The hedgehog is waiting to see if the stork will sob. This is giving the stork some trouble, it seems, but there's a fair outlook that he will manage it.

What a nocturnal comedy.

I could recount much else about the relationship of the stork to the hedgehog, but I mean to be moderate. The stork's situation vis-à-vis this scrap of deplorability seems deplorable. Why, too, does he allow himself to be moved so foolishly? Now tears are running down his ordinarily so judicious beak. Didn't I tell him it would be like this?

Is the hedgehog pleased about it?

That remains a secret. The nature of secrets is to be not explainable. The unexplainable is interesting. What is interesting is pleasing.

Stork! How art thou fallen!

Yet, on the other hand, you did fall for the dear and actually not insignificant hedgehog. What a privilege!

Have you ever seen a stork weep? You haven't? Well, that makes it so much the more curious.

In the stillness of night he weeps, not just buckets, but Niagaras. Grief for his adored hedgehog becomes for him a lasting need.

What's more, there's heroism in his yielding like this. A stork sometimes gets bored. Then off he goes and makes a hero of himself.

Dawn comes and still he stands there, in his never sufficiently commended agony. What patience.

To think that he has neglected, all this time, to bring children. Lord, the loss!

How the stork would have loved to kiss, with his beak, the spines of the hedgehog. What a kissing that would have been! We shudder at the thought of it.

[1925]

A Contribution

TO THE CELEBRATION OF

CONRAD FERDINAND MEYER

FLYING along streets that were swept almost to a shine, a jour-
nalist jotted into his unremittingly active global brain:
Fliers are flying in the blue above my head, which has no hat
on it, something I find beautiful and, at the same time, healthy.
I see a raw-materials truck and am astonished at my talent to
perceive the way a cavalier handles his umbrella, which once
belonged to the Duchess of Capulia. An official I identify by
the fact that, in the sunshine, he conceals his hands in his
trousers pockets. Some people do not dare to greet you, because they think it possible you might not return their courtesy.
An acquaintance of mine had expected me to display the
weakness of greeting him first. I refrained from doing so,
however, with an almost magnificent alacrity. He thereby sacri-
ficed the assurance of his conduct toward me, which conveyed
to me that he held me in esteem but did not want to advertise
it. As for me, it is this way: when I meet a person whom I
respect, I remove from my mouth, four meters before the encounter, the *Stumpen*, which is what we call a cigar hereabouts, I doff my cap and bow so subtly and inconspicuously
that there can be no possible doubt as to my showing esteem,
interpolation, every bit of it, and now I suddenly hear a gentleman say to his neighbor: "There goes one of those people

who are inclined to be not normal." A lady cyclist was carrying
a string bag full of vegetables and fruits. A girl was wearing
red high shoes, in impressive contrast to her white-stockinged
leg. In front of a hotel restaurant, where a governess is sitting
whom I am interested in, not that I have no interests in other
quarters, stands a wagon loaded with a big barrel, which might
contain nectar. A soft autumnal shimmer lies upon every street
and housefront. Hills on which vineyards are planted and evenings by lake shores arise before my lively mind's eye, together
with little dance halls in oak forests on islands. Perhaps I shall
lodge for three or four days in a country room with furniture of
the rococo period. Yet I doubt if I shall go there before com-
pleting, as I must, the present assignment. "*Quatre-vingt-
quatre*" now rings in my ears. I lot of French is spoken in our
city. In front of the municipal theater, a singer is arguing with
an actor. A little child smiles at me, but, with children, one
need not emphasize their smallness, because all children are
small, although, here and there, big ones exist, perhaps more
big ones than one is inclined to suppose.

Over lunch I read, in a newspaper favored by liberal thinkers, about a railway accident. I recall precisely that I ate lunch
only three hours ago. A poem is pursuing me; I shall have the
energy to write it down. When girls want to be noticed they
start to make arrangements with their hair; this can be perceived as a subtle challenge to spend one's time voluntarily
falling in love, but time is expensive, it wants to be used up to
the full. People without energy like to talk about energy. For
my part I am convinced that I have a quiet will of my own. Ah,
how distinctive she was, this servant girl leading a little boy by
the hand! Once I blew, to a nursemaid who stood for a superior
style of life, a kiss. The movement of her head told me: "Save
yourself the trouble." Often one is in somewhat too good a
mood. The houses today had such a beauty, a restraint, just
standing there, I can hardly find words for it. A poet, one of
those disturbers of genteel little drawing rooms, took his lady,
whom he idolized, by her tiny gloved hand and asked how she
had liked the verses which he had been quite understandably

saucy enough to send her. She answered, with a blush: "I was very glad, but please, meanwhile, let me go." For the simplicity of such language the poet appeared to have no perfect understanding such as she would have desired. I drew his attention to the reprehensibility, or impropriety, which, I said, seemed to me inherent in his behavior. While her molester was looking at me, the noble creature fled.

A city notable mumbled something in his beard; the beard was absent, but the expression is favored by many. Some turns of speech occur to us of their own accord. In a book-shop window shone, resplendent, the editions of a great poet. I refer to Conrad Ferdinand Meyer, the centenary of whose birth is being celebrated by the civilized world, which one might also call the impatient or rushing world. Civilization still seems to be an unfinished task. We shall always be vain about it, but never proud of it, and we shall never say that we have nothing more to learn, and we shall remember not only at the centenaries of famous poets the responsibilities which civilization lays upon us, and first and foremost when being civilized is our concern we shall not brag about it. To be sure, only the person who is always trying to be civilized is a civilized person, a person who is quite simply trying to be civilized, because that, if the truth were told, is not by any means so easy.

[1925]

A Sort of Speech

THIS deputy, how he pursued in metropolitan suburbs his irresponsibilities garnished all in green, afterwards casting deeply troubled glances at the ceiling, a consolation.

Certainly he'll have been a splendid father. We are the last who doubt the opulence of his somewhat pear-mellow noble intentions.

In the days of his youth he nodded with casual patience at the poets when they were introduced to him in his opera box.

As for his wife, her first mistake was to follow him zealously on the paths of his trespasses, thereby inviting him, deviously, to believe that he was very much loved by her.

Second, she was too involved with her brother, who could never be satisfied, on his solitary climbings, as morning breezes lisped around him, with mere medium heights.

So she was more of a sister than a wife and almost an egoist rather than a performer of her really very lovely duties. Above all, she was a beauty and never as long as she lived got over the idea.

Now to the sons, who carried jewelry caskets through woodlands by night, as if that were essential to them and their world.

One of them dreamed only of disappearing entirely from

sight. Often he must have read exciting stories. As a person, he was, in addition, nothing to speak of. So we shall dismiss him.

The second settled, as a recluse, in a villa which enshrouding ivy had rendered almost invisible.

The beard of this country-house dweller grew longer by the hour, until it extended out of the window, whereat he saw his life's task completed—a belief we gladly allow him.

The third found reason to become inconceivably incautious on account of a soprano, all naturally behind the wonderfully shaped back of his mother, who had a way of saying: "My sons displease me."

They made her suffer, she made them suffer, and the patriarch suffered from his spouse, and the products suffered because of the producers.

This family, to which many families looked up without reluctance, displayed a pompous falling short.

No pen can describe the sighs they heaved together.

Folly upon folly was committed.

What use is the most dazzling scenery?

The father knew no peace till he could say: "One darn thing after another!"

All the members of the family longed to be constantly wept over; the daughters found their language instructor bewitching.

Meanwhile, a book had been through many too many editions, a book which had the virtue of being nicely written. The book had melody.

The family we are speaking of had melody too.

There was a Mediterranean island in it, where the best opportunities for perceiving realities were dreamed away.

Still to this day it lies there, witness of a disinclination to wash oneself spiritually, in the proper way.

But they all wore fitting clothes and were virtuosos of dissatisfaction.

And then she who bore the responsibility might step forward and say to her son: "I command you to suffer!"

He laughed at her.

She says: "Get out of my sight!"—but wishes inwardly for him not to obey, she wrestles laboriously with her composure.

She feels guilty and innocent.

She blames the times.

"Tell me all! Vindicate yourself!"

He quietly replies: "All this longing to cast off the shackles, to despise what the surrounding world imposes upon you, isn't this what you're injecting into me? What you prohibit me from doing you should also deny yourself," and softly he adds: "Unbridled woman!"

Whereupon she has a scene with her husband.

If I felt talkative I'd repeat the reproaches she brought against him.

Her words slapped his face.

He thought it was very imposing to listen to her respectfully.

But his graciousness was for her a martyrdom.

Perhaps one can say that tact is the point from which powerlessness spreads more and more into the male world.

Defense to the last gasp seems to be not shrewd. If a man is shrewd, if he is conciliatory, relenting, submissive, the bonds are not torn, of course, but they still hang from him, more like threads, I mean as far as order is concerned, and women have won nothing, if one lets them win, although they tell themselves otherwise.

So he always eluded her, politely.

A reckless answer would have hurt her.

Together, by their fleeing from one another, they poisoned the atmosphere.

What kind of people am I thinking of, as I say this?

Of me, of you, of all our theatrical little dominations, of the freedoms that are none, of the unfreedoms that are not taken seriously, of these destroyers who never pass up a chance for a joke, of the people who are desolate?

Well, I could go around from person to person, letting each say some new thing, new but also old.

For they constantly repeated themselves. Each had his own sort of *idée fixe*.

And, in the theaters, plays were being performed that wearied the spectators' souls, made them rebellious and perverse, cringing, and eager for war.

Should one speak out or be silent?

[1925]

A Letter to
Therese Breitbach*

Bern, Thunstrasse 20/III
(mid-October 1925)

Rösi Breitbach, altogether most esteemed young lady! Wishing that you should show, if your feelings permit it, my letters to your parents, in all simplicity, generosity, and affection, I would like to tell you that for some time now I have not found anything here to write about, because I have already written so many things. I'm sure you'll understand this. Then I happened to read a small, silly sort of book, the kind you buy for a few cents at a kiosk, and it was most nicely entertaining to read it. I had read my fill of good books. Is it conceivable that you'll understand what I mean? If so, it would be most kind of you. All the girls here find me enormously boring, because they are all spoiled by zesty young bucks. Our masculine world can be very self-assured in its behavior. Once I took the liberty of sending, for instance, to a singer in our meritorious municipal theater, as token of my admiration, a copy of my book *Aufsätze*, published by Kurt Wolff. The book

* Therese Breitbach, with whom Walser exchanged letters between 1925 and 1932, was seventeen and living in Germany when she first wrote to Walser; they never met.

was returned, with the observation that I hadn't yet learned to write German. People hereabouts take me, generally, for an immature person, in every way. Even Thomas Mann, you know, that giant in the domain of the novel, regards me as a child, though a quite clever one to be sure. Once I was supposed to read from my work in Zurich, but the president of the Literary Circle which had invited me said that I had still not learned to speak German. For a time, people here thought I was insane, and would say aloud, in the arcades, as I was walking past: "He should be in the asylum." Our great Swiss writer, Conrad Ferdinand Meyer, whom you certainly know, also spent some time in a sanatorium for people who were mentally not altogether at their best. Now people are celebrating the centenary of this poor man's birth, with speeches and choral declamations. And yet once he no longer dared to take up his pen, in fear that he might botch everything he wrote. Then one day I went into a café and fell in love with a girl who looked so poetic. It was of course very foolish of me, all the utilitarians leaped upon me and reminded me of the bitter duties of my so lovely and expensive profession—which is of such a nature that it brings no money in. I loved this beautiful young girl, who seemed already to have an inclination toward corpulence, it was all because of the music I heard every day in the café. Great, indeed, is the power of music, sometimes immense. Suddenly everything changed. I made the acquaintance of a so-called *Saaltochter*, i.e., waitress, and from that moment the previous girl had for me in part only half a reality, in part no reality at all. Loving and what they call yearning are quite quite different things, different worlds. Then I used to go, very often, to nature, that is, walk into the country, many thoughts occurred to me, ideas, which I worked on. By doing this I left the place where the waitress served, and since then I haven't seen her; I subsequently wrote poems to her, and, well, there are many people around, also in your country, I expect, who think that poems are not work, but rather something comical, unworthy of respect. That has always been the case, and always will be, in Germany, the land of poets and thinkers. Our town is very lovely. Today I went swimming in deliciously cold water, soft and delicate sunshine, in the river which runs shimmering around our town like a serpent. Needless to say, nobody knows about the girl whom I made terrible fun of, partly in prose, and whom I worshipped, on the other hand, partly in poems. I have lived in rooms where all night I could not close my eyes for fear. Now it's like this: I no longer know for sure if I love her. Indeed, my dear Fraulein, one can keep one's feelings very much alive, or let them grow cold, neglect them. And then, true, I'm interested in many other matters besides. In the hope that you are happy, that your days pass pleasingly, and that you will be a little content, and perhaps also a bit dissatisfied, with this letter, I send you my cordial and of course, so to speak, respectful greetings.

Robert Walser

A Village Tale

I SIT down somewhat reluctantly at my desk to play my piano, that is to say, to begin to discourse on the potato famine which long ago struck a village on a hill that stood about two hundred meters high. Painfully I wrest from my wits a tale that tells of nothing of more account than a country girl. The longer she labored, the less she was able to do for herself.

The stars were twinkling in the sky. The parson of the village where what is here told occurred was out of doors elucidating for his young protégés the planetary system. A writer was working in a lamplit room at his rapidly waxing work when, vexed by visions, the girl rose up from her bed intending to rush into the pond, which she did with almost laughable alacrity.

When she was found the next morning in a condition which made it plain to all that she had ceased to live, the question rose among these countryfolk: Should she be buried or not. Not a soul was ready to lay a hand on the finished article that lay quite motionless there. Tribal displeasure asserted itself.

The bailiff approached the group, which intrigued him primarily from the viewpoint of painting, for in his leisure hours he would paint, government burdening him with no excessive duties. He urged the country people forthwith to be sensible, but his expostulations had no success; at no price would they inter the girl, as if they believed it might harm them to do so.

The sheriff strode into his office with its three large windows through which streamed the most dazzling light, and he wrote a report on the incident which he dispatched to the city authorities.

But what feelings assail me when I consider the famine whose waves rose higher and higher! The populace grew unspeakably thin. How they longed for food!

The very same day a laborer of superlative efficiency took his gun from its nail and shot, with authentic popular wrath, his rival who was crossing the street below, yodeling in all innocence, clear proof of how happy his days were. In fact the rival was just returning from a successful encounter with the young lady, who seemed to be a somewhat indecisive person, for ogling both she offered prospects to both of heaven.

Never in all my years as a writer have I written a tale in which a person, struck by a bullet, falls down. This is the first time in my work that a person has croaked.

Understandably, they lifted him up and carried him into the next-best cottage. Houses, in the present comfortable sense of the word, did not at that time exist in the country; there were only indigent dwellings, whose roofs of straw reached almost to the ground, as one may still observe, at one's leisure, in a few surviving examples.

When the young lady, a country belle with swaying hips and a taut, tall body, heard what had occurred on her account, she simply stood there, bolt upright, pondering deeply perhaps her peculiar nature.

Her mother besought her to speak, but all in vain; it seemed she had been changed into a statue.

A stork flew through the azure air high over the village drama, bearing in its beak a baby. Wafted by a slight wind, the leaves whispered. Like an etching it all looked, anything but natural.

[1927]

The Aviator

A PERSON who wishes to voice a conviction in an appropriate fashion pronounces a vigorous, martial "Naturaleh!" "With martial greetings I remain your most obedient servant" —thus did I close a letter to someone who avowed to me that my martialism had taken him aback. "All of a sudden he heard somebody beside him exclaim: 'That's impossible!' " Couldn't such an ordinary event as this occur in a novel that reflects its times and speaks of matters that are perhaps largely marginal issues? If I now exclaim in a booming voice "Naturaleh!"—I have in mind the artist of aviation who, with an energy to be wondered at, flew across the ocean; and of course I number myself among the innumerable people who revere this happy dominator of difficulties. A person who has no doubts at all about anything is prone to asseverate: "It's clear as day!" That the aviator mounting his vehicle seemed to himself tiny in proportion to the magnitude of his task is clear as day to me, and perhaps I might be permitted to believe that in this significant moment he was lulling himself into the conceivably very artful illusion of being, in comparison with the universe, a babe in arms, and his flying machine was his crib, where the most decisive thing for him to do was to lie low, quietly watching. In my opinion, during the truly fabulous unwinding of his journey

he thought most animatedly of his mother. Of this I am convinced, and now I come face to face with the question: Should
one view the oceanist, the hero of the day, as a descendant of
those mariners vanished long since from their sphere of influence, and furthermore did he, before he flew off, make it his
precept to consider his enterprise as something that would, so
to speak, be merely a schooling for him, an education? Especially a poet does well, among other things, to fly at a modest
velocity on his winged steed, Pegasus by name, because ill
chance may strike the most special person no less easily than
the least consequential member of any human interest group or
sphere. Today I told myself that in actual fact anyone who
takes an innocuous and random delight in his life is an absolute
lummox.

As regards this appellation, which disconcertingly took wing
from my otherwise so choice vocabulary, it seems I should
explain that it denotes a low-down sort of character. By lummox, one should understand a fusion of every conceivable in-
eptitude in the person of a particular social fellow being. With
a splendid, because moderate, velocity I strode today, as it
happens, into a shoe solery to ask what steps had been taken,
what progress made, toward finishing work in which I knew I
had an interest. Instead of saying "lummox," in a country that
delights in its reputation for hospitality and where, besides
which, I too am permitted to live, some folks make use of the
designation *dummer Cheib*, or fathead. Neither the latter nor
the former manner of speaking sounds polite; both shed a certain uncultivated dimness upon persons who put them to use.
Like a bird of paradise he flew across the far-flung and not by
any means entirely bland and composed carpet of meadows
historically called the sea, the fool or lummox, who may be
called a lummox insofar as he was gambling, so audaciously as
to be well-nigh presumptuous, with the indisputable treasure of
his life, on which apparently, since he was thus exposing it to
all vicissitudes, he placed little value, in a manner which was,
well now, how should one put it, almost indiscreet; for surely
one may be right to think that a person who commits himself to

the discharge of a duty, a general human concern, and thereby shows little or no regard for his own person, is in equal proportions a tall and broad, perhaps even towering, lummox or fathead? On the other hand, I can see in him someone who empowers himself to inhale and exhale the glory and delight of life, for when enjoyment, meaning the principle of healthy egoism, is set aside, then precisely does the richer and purer source of what is initially disdained begin. The careless or selfless person, it is my conviction, does persistently care for himself, although I am ready at any moment to admit the contradictoriness here apparent, which, in itself, is of great significance for me.

When, for instance, someone becomes self-important, it is popularly said that he has "a bee in his bonnet." A person can be just as important as he pleases, in fact; but to appear so is not always pleasant for others.

In the finer sense, as in the one just indicated, I launch toward you, somewhat like a bee, the present essay.

[1927]

The Pimp

WHAT an irreparable error it would be, if to the high pile of errors that during my lifetime have slipped from me, as if hatched from eggs of misconception, I were to add that of declaring this house somewhere on a hilltop to be a palace, seeming as it did more like a villa or pavilion, a neat little convalescent home, where, as a lackey, for I could not have figured there as anything loftier or better, I performed tasks that were in my opinion of preeminent quality, although I cannot but realize that my manner of speaking is rather long-winded.

Even if I saw that my employer—I do not know if I should be saying this—sometimes indulged her habit of pressing together her unspeakably thin lips, still she was for me the world's most beautiful woman, while it would never have occurred to me to extol her as a miracle of rare proportions, to which reality did give me every imaginable reason.

The mountain ridge upon which one looked across from one of the surely very numerous windows had a very pleasant face, by which I would like to have intimated that it was a joy to devote to it a proper measure of the attention it well deserved. Oh, the freedom, the finesse, of which it was, from afar, seeming to be at once both far and near, a perfect expression! I thought I could touch the mountain with my hands; in any event, its stoninesses had the effect of a face that responded, in content as in form, to each and every demand.

Days and days went by before I could somewhat orient myself as to what sort of business the delightfully located house, ringed around as it was, so to speak, with little dancings, might be based upon. What very remarkable purpose did it serve? More than once, this was my question.

Unbelievably diffuse festivities spreading out for as long as one could wish over fabulously beautiful gardens and lasting from first light, each time so graceful it was like a goddess awakening, far into the dusk and longer still, to the edge of night, were lavished in the countryside in which this estate stood, proud as a temple and yet modest in every way, on all who wished to have a share in a healthy and thus worthwhile experience, some of whom had been invited by word of mouth, some in writing.

That the meadows, enlivened here and there most charmingly by trees, were of a green to the intensity of which even the most intense grumblers, and to the gaiety of which even the most innate peeves, could raise little if any objection, is almost certain to be as good as obvious.

The house was thronged with well-disciplined girls, vying with one another as regards their proper tasks, which is probably the best and most civil thing to be said about human apparitions clad generally in aprons and equipped with feathered dust absorbers.

From time to time I heard my beautiful and doubtless much beleaguered employer exclaim in quite a loud voice: "Don't put me on edge!" To what species of earth dweller did she say this? Naturally for me it could only remain for a long time an inscrutable riddle, whose insolubility was like a sumptuous garment, of which I became, so to speak, enamored.

One thing I may and must mention with due care. In the garden which, bordered to the south perhaps by a stream that propelled itself with extraordinary gentleness along its course, and extending northward into a most motley hilliness, there was, like a bouquet of flowers, a multitude of delicious nooks, which really did appear like friendly little faces, and where, at one's pleasure, that is to say, most freely, one could lark about, take a rest, make a little love—saying which reminds me that kind fate, of which I have undertaken never to complain, since that would not, in my opinion, be appropriate, once led me into a theater to share the spectacle of a play which simultaneously delighted me and left me somewhat dissatisfied. Might I confess to finding that it is exquisite to be of two minds regarding works of art? To find fault with something that I welcome on the whole, how nice I find this is!

As regards the blossoming trees in the garden, I allow myself the liberty of using the epithet "enchanting," and of the owner, the person, that is to say, who was entitled to claim, with regard to all the beauty I have described, "You are mine," it will be desirable to mention, with a sort of horrified dismay in the voice with which I say it, the fact that he was a pimp, whom the most substantial connections seemingly contrived to make undetectable.

How winning his appearance was, and how fetchingly he knew how to move about always in the most decorous society, standing out and striding around as one of the most artful seducers of the century, and who, one day, as the air was just beginning to shade into vesperal violet, was walking in my company on steep paths down the mountain, accordingly as an individual whose overcoat I obediently carried, and who suddenly, before my very eyes, in the middle of an old walkway, sank into an abyss that opened at his feet, sank with all his elegant sinuosities, confusing inexplicabilities, like a figure on a stage, simply vanishing.

A woman of the middle class who saw the drama, too, exclaimed in a shrill voice: "Serves him right!" Never shall I forget the curt, bolt-upright way in which this original, i.e., completely singular member of human society, dropped into the downrightest sawn-offness.

Ready, set—and that was the end of him. Mantled in thought, I returned to the house. The estimable gentleman's overcoat was a showpiece of the garment industry.

"She was spellbound by him," I believed myself entitled to whisper, thinking the light that had dawned on me not too bright, and first smoking a subtly fragrant cigarette.

It was one of his.

[1927]

Masters and Workers

T HERE are not many things that I want to say on the subject of masters and workers. The problem cuts deeply into
conditions at the present time, which appear positively to
seethe with beings who are workers and who sometimes disregard this particular fact. Don't we sometimes dream with our
eyes open, see blindly, feel without feeling, listen without hearing, and don't we often, when walking, stand still? What a
succession of quiet, solid, honorable questions!

Approach, you real barons, that I may discern the linea-
ments of veritable master types! Masters, to me, are quite a
priceless rarity, and a master is, in my view, a man who is
touched now and again by the curious need to forget that he is
a master. Whereas the workers are distinguished by the way
they please to fancy themselves masters, the masters on occasion look down upon them, envying in an understandable sort
of way the gaieties and frivolities of the workers; for it seems to
me an indubitable fact that the masters are the lonely ones,
insofar as they are perpetually in the right and therefore crave
to learn what it tastes and smells like to be in the wrong, a
thing they cannot know. The masters can behave as they
please; not the workers, who consequently never cease longing
for command, which they lack, though it could be said to the
contrary that the masters are often fed to the teeth with their

directordom, would rather be serving and obeying than issuing decrees, the activity in which they see their lives most monotonously absorbed.

"How I'd love one day to get a really good ticking-off!"—it's a wish that could easily occur, in my opinion, to this or that master, whereas the workers know nothing of suchlike wishes, which are never fulfilled. It's not only wealth that makes a master; likewise, on the other hand, a worker doesn't need to be a poor downtrodden wretch. A master, I'm convinced, is what he is much more because it is he who answers requests, just as a worker is what he thinks he is because it is from his lips that requests ring out. The worker waits; the master keeps people waiting. Yet waiting can sometimes be just as pleasant, or even more so, than keeping waiting, which requires strength. A person waiting can afford the sweet luxury of being in no way responsible; while he waits, he can think of his wife, his children, his mistress, and so on; of course, the person who keeps people waiting can do this too, if it gives him any pleasure. But it can happen that the nondescript who is waiting absolutely refuses to get off his mind, and naturally that's a burden.

"This dependent of mine may now be smiling to himself with extraordinary placidity," he thinks; and he'd gladly expire with a magisterial wrath which almost puts him out of countenance; and that such an incomprehensible kind of wrath should be possible at all belongs among the perils of the master's state. A master frequently ought to be something like a superman, yet still he remains a man, a fellow man, and "Damnation!" he shouts, fearing for himself, as it were. "Hasn't he been waiting long enough, this man, martyrizing me with his patience?" And he presses the bell button; that's to say, he gives the button a bash, and sees in an instant the fatuity of his explosion. He snubs an incoming zealot with a melodramatic brutality that should be seen, and he would happily devour, tigerlike, the sheep who's waiting for his masterednesses and self-composures, and instead of dropping destructively on an enervating nonentity he jumbles up papers that seem to be giving him a professional look, in a daze, as if they were poor sinners, and the worker has no idea what's got into the master who is offended to be capable of a sentiment, who is insulted to be able now and again to be unhappy, who is emotionally almost demolished to be regarded as a demolisher, which he is not, doesn't want to be, cannot be.

"Let me help you!" They're most often unspeakably good-humored, the people who write such turns of speech, and an incredibly bad mood can possess a person who has occasion to write: "I readily assume that such and such has been promptly dealt with."

Obeying and commanding commingle; good manners rule masters as well as workers. I offer this essay workerishly and regard its peruser as a master to whom I wish acquaintance with the gratification of seeing some chance to prize what I give him.

My theme does meddle somewhat, of course, as if it came too close to life, which may perhaps have grown too sensitive. What made life so? Is it going to stay as it is, or change? Why am I asking this? Why do so many questions come to me, softly, one after the other? I know, for instance, that I can live without questions. I lived without them for a long time, knew nothing of them. I was open-minded, without their invading me. Now they look at me as if I had an obligation to them. I too, like many people, became sensitive. Time is sensitive, like a person begging for help, a person perplexed. The questions beg and are sensitive and insensitive. The sensitivities harden. The disobliged person is perhaps the most sensitive. Obligations make me, for instance, hard. Those who are begged beg the beggars, who don't understand this. The questions gaze solicitously in upon them, and are not solicitous, and those who take care of them care for the increase of the questions which regard their answerers as being insensitive. The person who'll not let them disturb his equanimity for an instant is sensitive in their sight. In that they appear to him answered, he answers them. Why do many people not trust them this way?

[1928]

Essay on Freedom

PUTTING on airs, playing squeamish, acting sensitive, shilly-shallying, finessing, fussing, and frequent dreaming in the night, all this too appertains to freedom, which one can never, in my opinion, comprehend, sense, consider, and respect variously enough. One should always be bowing inwardly to the pure image of freedom; there must be no pause in one's respect for freedom, a respect which seems to bear a persistent relation to a kind of fear. A remarkable thing here is that freedom sets out to be single, tolerates no other freedoms beside itself. Although this can certainly be said with greater precision, I quickly take occasion to insist that I am a person who tends to appear to himself more frail than he perhaps actually is.

For instance, I allow myself to be positively governed by freedom, so to speak oppressed by it, to be regulated by it in every imaginable way, and with a constancy that amuses me there dwells within me a most outspoken distrust of it, admirable though it be, this freedom, which I almost refrain from mentioning at all. —Freedom smiles at me, and what in turn do I do but say to myself: "Mind you, don't let yourself be seduced by this smile into all sorts of unprofitabilities."

I return now to nocturnal dreams, whose main intent, in my

opinion, is to intimidate us. The dreams make the free person aware of the dubieties, limits, or provisos of freedom, especially of its being a beautiful delusion which needs to be handled in the most delicate way. Perhaps for this reason not many people know how to deal with freedom correctly, because they do not wish to become accustomed to allowing for its violability. A delusion quickly flits away; we easily contrive to make the fantasm, as it were, hate us, because we do not understand what it essentially is. Freedom wants both to be understood and to be almost continuously not understood; it wants to be seen and then again to be as if it were not there; it is at once real and unreal, and on this point much more might well be said. Last night I dreamed among other things of quite remarkable advances being made to me by a person from whom I had never, never expected anything of the sort. Enchanting it is, the way dreams can mock the sleeper, the way they flutter the brain with freedoms which, on waking, seem laughable.

With the reader's leave, or rather that of the readeress, whom the writer always pictures as a lovely person, well-disposed, I draw attention, with a humility which cannot of course be free from decorous irony, to the droll possibility that, within freedom, puzzles are thinkable. One evening I start off homeward and on arriving at the house where I live I see two people, a man and a woman, looking out of the window of my room. Both these unknown people have conspicuously large faces and are quite motionless, a sight possibly apt to make a free person unfree on the spot, in every way. For quite a long time he stares at the people staring, so to speak nonchalantly, down at him, he cannot explain to himself their presence, goes upstairs, intending to ask the inexplicable occupants of his room, as politely as possible, to tell him, if they would be so kind, why they are there, and I walk in, find everything quiet, no persons are there. For a time I do not sense my own person either, I am pure independence, which is not in every way quite what it ought to be, and I ask myself if I am free.

Isn't there a beautiful woman I know who remarks, every

time I meet her, that I do not please her, because once I did please her but apparently was not able to feel fortunate enough about it? She is a free woman, and consequently a sensitive one, who feels every insensitivity most sensitively, who in other words considers every freedom one allows oneself to take regarding her to be unrefined and partly forfeits her candor, that is, her freedom, which, as I believe I have been able to stress, has about it much that is not understood, never experienced, constantly astonishing, warming and chilling, something that is troubled by any failure to consider how it is constituted.

I hope I may be believed if I permit myself to say that freedom is difficult and produces difficulties, with which phrase perhaps there sprang from my mouth an insight the expression of which could be accomplished by none but a connoisseur and gourmet of freedom who notes and cherishes all the unfreedoms internal to freedom.

[1928]

A Biedermeier Story

Iɴ the Biedermeier period, thus during the time when, let's say, a Lenau brought to the shaping stage his ineffably delicate and beautiful verses, at his ease, and slowly, as he raised them up out of the silent depths of not yet having been written down, there lived, unless my presence of mind forsakes me entirely, a housemaid, of whom and in whose hearing, albeit she was in her way an excellent person perhaps, more young than old, and more nearly beautiful than fundamentally hideous, some were apt to say she was a beast.

If her hair was a fair match for her eyes, she also enjoyed the not particularly nice reputation of being a glutton, which could have been an insult, of such utterly unwarranted slightness that, living, moving, and standing as I do in my own epoch, I am most gratifyingly astonished by it.

During the time when, as is well known, the Russian general Gorchakov practically dominated the European scene, there existed with the upper and lower middle class, to set ladies' maids' fingers flying, corsets, or bodices. Everyone knows that Biedermeier women were laced to the utmost tightness when they went to their soirées.

The moment this housemaid, due to the prevailing servant hierarchy, received a blow on the head, she would say of the punishment that had been inflicted upon her, yes, insofar as she would smile politely, that is to say, with impertinent civility.

She worked in a nimble way, but her lover became, with more success than was welcome to his fellows, a criminal, who did with wondrous precision things I shall not mention.

While misdeed upon misdeed accrued to his credit, or, in slightly differient language, good prose pieces galore seemed to drop from his pen, his conduct toward the housemaid was so beneficial that she believed she was right to think of him as a man whose goodness had no bounds.

The maid, true, though this emphasis is only incidental, had a habit of eating *Schabziger*, as they call it, a variety of herb cheese. More and more difficult did it become for him to kiss her on the lips. He once took the risk of indicating disapproval thereof; she begrudged him this.

With a nobly casual air as befitted his rank as a war lord, General Gorchakov, who only comes into this sketch of mine for local color, commanded his armies.

Once the housemaid had performed her tasks, instead of going out for a walk, which certainly would have done her no harm, she went to her room, sat down at the table, and started to write.

If it was letters she wrote that reached her lover safely every time, perhaps the window was open and a sparrow, or chaffinch, would be fluttering on the sill.

All the songs of singing birds heard by people such a long, long time ago!

[1928–29]

The Honeymoon

IT was ideal, and the couple would think of it for a long time afterwards. He wore on his head a beret and she a *voile de voyage* floating in the wind that scudded over the blades of grass. The forest edge checked the wind. Firs waved and nodded, and good-naturedly oaks spread their limbs. "We hope with hearts as one," he said. She looked at him, gratefully. In their rolling motor car they came into a sumptuous town with high-gabled houses glowing duskily. Among the splendid, exquisite buildings were blossoming gracious trees that seemed to bid the new arrivals welcome. On the windowsills flowerpots stood, and in the inn where the couple comfortably dismounted, for repast and repose, musicians were fluting, bagpiping, and trumpeting. The next day their journey took them across fields and through forests. Beside a sparkling brook, as it rippled along, they had a snug idyllic picnic in a setting of distant hills. Traveling on, they encountered a crackpot who, gaunt and very tall, in threadbare lackadaisical clothes, gave them a haughty look. "Bachelor!" said the bridegroom, suffused with love and devotion, to the stranger, "why do you look at us with such contempt?" The scornful smiler answered: "Because I am nagging and caviling at you, and only half believe in your happiness." The bride shook her head, as if this man who doubted joy was beyond her comprehension. Soon the philosophical figure had disappeared from their sight. In time they came to a station, through which a train passed. Not far from there a friendly body of water spread itself, in a wreath of reeds. A swan was swimming on the calm, clear surface. From a bell tower on whose tip a cockerel shone golden in the sun, a clock announced the hour. A boy on stilts strutted past a table on whose top a pair of gloves was lying. A Gaul or Hun had a tobacco pipe in his mouth and was belaboring with a saw a piece of wood, using a sawing horse. For a time the eyes of the happy couple were attracted to a spindle. A hunter pursued a partridge, aided by a nimble and willing dog. Toward the swan, on the lake shore, a pig walked at a leisurely pace, grunting contentedly from time to time, aiming to cozy up to the noble creature. The ill-favored animal, which even then presented a sort of image of peerlessness, succeeded in coming up alongside. The swan, in its soft and elegant way, was willing to accommodate the eager pig in partnership. What a beautiful thing friendship can be! Yet many other sights were in store for them, a farmer plowing, for instance, and next to him a country manor of townlike appearance, over which a snail was strolling, on some errand or other, if to speak of a stroll can be justified here. A robed rider rode on his buoyant horse out of a suggestive thicket, evidently on a mission, and a piece of rope, or string, was lying on a bench. The bench was absorbed in the expectation of being sat on. To enumerate every concrete thing in the world would exhaust me, and the reader too, so I shall confine myself and wish the couple a safe return home and a cornucopia of delights on their life's way. All around they looked, were interested in a variety of things, took careful note of some, including an elephant, a dove, and a snake. Capped with fluttering bannerets, and highbreasted, a ship ran into a harbor. Barrels and boxes lay there in quiet heaps. Before a group of soldiers, someone who had made a mistake and was about to atone for it received a number of blows, buffets, or lashes. The person inflicting the punishment stood at attention, while the recipient of it kneeled and implored, quite properly, for trustful behavior did not suit him. Over him as he whimpered, a crocodile was shedding tears. Little swallows flew through the blue over an acrobat competing with a juggler who threw balls, torches, knives, and so forth, into the air, each attempting to astonish with his art, with finesse and winsomeness. Twenty meters and more above the earth an angel sat, as if on a chair. How did he do so, without any basis? There was nothing to support him, sustain him; nevertheless, he sat there, with peace of mind, angelic, absolving an exercise. The friendly expression never left his face for a second. Not a trace of strain did he show. Apparently he could do this difficult thing with perfect ease. A fullness evidently fortified and secured him. And he never ate anything! Food makes one feel tired, crusty, heavy, stiff, and somnolent. In fasting there is unquestionably a deep significance, an impulse, a lifting up. A task had taken possession of the angel; he had been entirely absorbed into it. A will to attain an object, to merge with the object, to become one with it, to be himself, filled him. I could never do what he could. For him it was the opposite. Not to be able to do what he had to do would not have been possible for him. Thus he sat there so peacefully, so dead.

"When I am dead," said the bride to her bridegroom, "my life will be stronger, better, because then you will think of me all the time."

Home again, they talked about the curiosities their journey had revealed to them, on a balcony. A sunshade was spread over the charming lady.

The work he meant to devote himself to was already claiming his thoughts, and he had fears for himself, because he was doubtful about his enterprise, and for her, because he intended to forsake her somewhat.

Had his happiness come so soon to stand in his way?

[1928–9]

Thoughts on Cézanne

IF one chose to, one might notice a lack of bodiliness; but outline is the principal thing, long years, perhaps, of concern for the object. The man I'm now speaking of gazed, for instance, at these fruits, which are as ordinary as they are remarkable, for a long time; he pondered their look, the skin stretched taut around them, the strange repose of their being, their laughing, glowing, good-humored appearance. "Isn't it well-nigh tragic," he might have said to himself, "that they cannot be conscious of their use and beauty?" He would have liked to communicate, to infuse, to transmit into them his capacity for thought, because he was sorry for them, on account of their being unable to have any conception of themselves. I feel convinced that he commiserated with them, and then again with himself, and that for a long time he really did not know why.

Even this tablecloth has its own peculiar soul, so he wished to imagine, and every related wish came true, at once. Pale, white, enigmatically pure it lay there: he walked up to it, rumpled it. Amazing how it let itself be grasped, exactly as the person touching it had desired. It may be that he spoke to it: "Come to life!" Meanwhile, one should not forget that he had the necessary time to undertake strange experiments, exercises, playful tests, investigations. He was fortunate to have a wife to whom he could entrust, without any anxiety, everyday cares, housekeeping, etc. He seems to have treated her as a large and beautiful flower that never opened its cup, her lips, to utter the least complaint. Oh, this flower, it kept to itself everything about him that displeased her, she was, I tell myself, a miracle of docility, her tolerance of her husband's quirks and circumspections was the tolerance of an angel. The latter were for her a magic palace, which she left alone, approved of, into which she never penetrated with the least innuendo, of which she thought little, though she also respected it. She could tell herself: These matters are no concern of mine. Doubtless because she never did impinge upon her companion's mere "schoolboy difficulties," which is how his efforts often appeared to her, she had humanity, or shall we say tact. For hours and days on end he sought out ways to make unintelligible the obvious, and to find for things easily understood an inexplicable basis. As time went by, a secret watchfulness settled in his eyes from so much precise circling of contours that became for him edges of a mystery. An entire quiet lifetime he spent fighting inaudibly and, one might be tempted to say, with nobility, to make mountainous—if such a paraphrase might suffice—the frame of things.

My gist is that a region, for instance, becomes bigger and richer in a surround of mountains.

Apparently his wife did often try to persuade him that he should relinquish the gallings of this almost ridiculous struggle, that he should travel somewhere, not be so deeply absorbed all the time in such a singular and monotonous task.

He replied: "All right! Might I ask you to do the necessary packing?"

She did so, yet he didn't travel, but stayed where he was, that is to say, he traveled and raveled again in circles around the limits of the bodies he portrayed, the bodies he reconstructed, and from the bag or basket she removed again, just as gently, and somewhat thoughtfully, everything she had packed with the utmost care into them, and the same old life went on as before, the old life that this dreamer renewed for himself again and again.

One might keep an eye on the peculiarity that he looked upon his wife as if she were a fruit on the tablecloth. For him the outlines, the contours of his wife were exactly the same simple but also complicated ones as he'll have seen around flowers, glasses, dishes, knives, forks, tablecloths, fruits, and coffeepots and cups. A pat of butter was for him just as significant as a delicate pleat corrugating his wife's dress. I recognize that my wording here is inadequate, but I would like to think that I can be understood nevertheless, or perhaps better and more deeply, on account of such provisional phrasing, in which the lights have a shimmering effect, although I deplore in principle, of course, any sort of hastiness. He persisted in being that kind of studio person who is always open to attack from the standpoint of family or nation. One can hardly refrain from believing that he was Asiatic. Is not Asia the motherland of art, of spirituality, these utter luxuries? To think of him as a person who never liked to eat would probably be mistaken. He ate fruits and studied them with equal pleasure; he enjoyed the taste of ham just as much as its form and color, which he called "wonderful," and its presence, which he called "phenomenal." If he drank wine, its pleasant taste astonished him—though one should not speak exaggeratedly of this characteristic. For he translated wine, too, into the domain of art. He magicked flowers onto paper, so that upon it they quivered, rejoiced, and smiled, swaying in their plantlike ways; his concern was the flesh of flowers, the spirit of the secret which dwells in the resistance a thing with special properties offers to understanding.

All the things he grasped became intermarried, and if we find it proper to speak of his musicality, it was from the plenitude of his observation that it sprang, and from his asking each object if it might agree to give him a revelation of its essence, and most preeminently from his placing in the same "temple" things both large and small.

The things he contemplated became eloquent, and the things to which he gave shape looked back at him as if they had been pleased, and that is how they look at us still.

One could justly insist that he made the most extensive use, bordering on the inexhaustible, of the suppleness and the compliance of his hands.

[1929]

Postscript

Robert Walser (1878–1956) wrote four novels during his thirty years as a writer. Three were published during the first decade of this century (1906, 1907, 1908) and attracted some remarkable minds, notably Morgenstern and Kafka, but they hardly appealed to a broad public. The fourth novel was lost in the early 1920s. Eventually, the manuscript surfaced in West Berlin and was published as *Der Räuber-Roman* in 1976. It is in the field of short prose that Walser excelled. There is some justice to his claim to be writing, in separate swirls of short prose, a "long, plotless, realistic story," but his clownish and distinctly Swiss genius was at its best in miniature fictions with a rapid pulse—those sketches, soliloquies, improvisations, arabesques, and capriccios that form his ten collections (1904–25) and the four volumes of uncollected work now available in the *Gesamtwerk*.

Walser was largely self-educated, always poor, and just as dedicated to his mischievously secret and independent life as Rilke was to his forbidding "work." Among the various types of short prose in the German tradition, going back to the medieval Latin *Gesta Romanorum*, there are certain strains which, like the ballad and the folk song, escape those distinctions that have historically tended to reserve certain other genres for readers of the upper or middle classes (e.g., the novel). Small wonder that Walser, with his proletarian mode of life and his princely imagination, found in short prose his proper habitat.

As for the tradition, one thinks of the anecdotes that pepper Abraham a Sancta Clara's sermons of the seventeenth century; of philosophical aperçus from Lichtenberg to Nietzsche and Wittgenstein; of Johann Peter Hebel's tales and reports of the early 1800s; of the Expressionist "grotesques" of Salomo Friedländer (preceded by the fantasies of Josef Popper-Lynkeus); and, by no means least, of the nineteenth- and early twentieth-century masters of *feuilleton*, the miniature impressions, gossipings, entertainments, anecdotes, parables, often with a lyrical twist, which since the 1820s—following French models—had been appearing under the main news items on the front page of newspapers. All this was the humus out of which eventually Walser's short prose came; out of the same humus came, too, Kafka's Yggdrasill of parables.

Walser eked out a living as a feuilletonist, contributing also to periodicals, in Berlin (1905–13), in Biel (1913–20), and in Berne (1921–32). Yet his prose surpasses, in coloration and sensibility, the usual sketch or impression of the time. What I have tried to do in this selection is present some of the main lines, or radiations, of his power of invention in the miniature, of his charm in the grotesque, also of his ironic reflexivity, viz., his jazzy oscillations between levels of discourse—dense and transparent, straight and mocking. Conceivably, he was one of the earliest and foremost artists in German prose to make positive fun of his understanding that the truth of writing can deregulate or negate reference, while seeming to uphold it. Well before the 1920s, the text for Walser is a non-thing, as much so as a Cubist guitar or Magritte's apple (*"Ceci n'est pas une pomme"*).

The only period missing from the selection is the earliest one, about 1898–1904. Some of *Fritz Kochers Aufsätze* might have been included, also an early miniature play, or "dramolet" —Walter Benjamin thought *Schneewitzchen* profound and exemplary. At least in "Helbling" and "The Little Berliner" the reader will find amplified versions of Fritz Kocher, the impish schoolboy soliloquist who, not much later, becomes the *Kommis*, or clerk, as underdog, whose character as Walser portrayed him captured Kafka's imagination.

Walser did not stop writing when he voluntarily entered the Waldau mental hospital in Berne in 1929. It was only when he was forcibly transferred to Herisau in Appenzell, in 1933, that he gave up, or switched, one might say, from being an incalculable alien to being an official lunatic. His last "sane" book publication was *Die Rose*, in 1925; but throughout the 1920s he was writing prolifically, at times frenetically, and always with gusto, in his extraordinary solitude. To Jochen Greven we are indebted for the recovery and deciphering of hundreds of prose miniatures from that period. These now appear, together with pieces that were published in newspapers and journals, in the four posthumous volumes, *Festzug*, *Phantasieren*, *Olympia*, and *Der Europäer*. From these books I have chosen several texts; datings come from the same source.

To some extent Robert Walser was, in Artaud's phrase, "suicided by society." Certainly he was one of the great European artists in language, since Christopher Smart, to have risked all rather than compromise, and to have been broken eventually, like Hölderlin, perhaps, or Nerval, by certain neurochemical effects of a demonic anguish. (Yet, in his madness, Walser was surprisingly sane. To Carl Seelig, who became his legal guardian in the late 1930s, he once said, when asked if he was writing anything: "I am not here to write, but to be mad.") Altogether, one reads Walser for his blithe difference from colleagues in any age or any condition—for his perfect and serene oddity. He composes a language that is prodigiously his own, even when the words in their structures tally with Swiss German and High German. The translators have done their best. Speaking for myself, I have taken few liberties and those only to mark the whirling track of Walser's dance more clearly in English than might otherwise have been the case (also perhaps more quaintly than some solemn readers might relish).

The Walk and Other Stories (1957) has been taken up into the present book, with some revisions. Acknowledgment is made to John Calder for permission to reprint the four texts in that book. Acknowledgment is made also to the little magazines in which Tom Whalen, having discovered Walser in the forests of Arkansas and made of him, later, a sort of hero for some very gifted young writers in New Orleans, placed his collaborative translations: *Barataria, Chowder Review, Lowlands Review, The Paris Review, Writ*; to *Delos*, in which Harriett Watts's translation first appeared (1968); and to *Texas Quarterly*, in which "Helbling's Story" and "Masters and Workers" appeared (1964). Walser's third novel, *Jakob von Gunten* (University of Texas Press, 1969), might appeal to readers who have enjoyed this selection. For a brilliant, imaginative reconstruction of Robert Walser, as a spirit touching fingertips with Erik Satie, the reader is referred to Guy Davenport's "A Field of Snow on a Slope of the Rosenberg," in his book *Da Vinci's Bicycle*.

Christopher Middleton